FORGIVENESS

James A. Michener Fiction Series

JAMES MAGNUSON, EDITOR

Forgiveness

BY JIM GRIMSLEY

University of Texas Press ⌄ Austin

Requests for permission to reproduce material from this work
should be sent to:
    Permissions
    University of Texas Press
    P.O. Box 7819
    Austin, TX 78713-7819
    www.utexas.edu/utpress/about/bpermission.html

∞ The paper used in this book meets the minimum requirements
of ANSI/NISO39.48–1992 (R1997) (Permanence of Paper).

Library of Congress Cataloging-in-Publication Data
Grimsley, Jim, 1955–
Forgiveness / by Jim Grimsley. — 1st ed.
        p.   cm. — (The James A. Michener fiction series)
ISBN-13: 978-0-292-71669-8 ((cl.) : alk. paper)
ISBN-10: 0-292-71669-9
1. Psychological fiction. 2. Domestic fiction. I. Title.
PS3557.R4949F67 2007
813'.54—dc22   2006022582

For Lisa Corley

Contents

FORGIVENESS

My Lifetime Movie Begins

TODAY I SAW AN SUV drive up the side of a building, climbing to the very top where a helicopter was landing. This was a TV commercial, of course, but looked completely real. A man stepped out of the SUV and kissed his wife good-bye. She sat, relaxed, her hair ruffled by the helicopter, behind the steering wheel. She had a beautiful face, sandy hair, but beyond that I could see only her shoulders and the shapes of her breasts under her blue cotton blouse. She had a pretty smile. Her husband climbed into the helicopter and she drove down the side of the building. I believe she was driving on a skyscraper somewhere in Manhattan. The woman smiled like a perfect wife. My own wife wants a divorce. I have decided to kill her, but I'm not sure how.

She has long ago ceased to be beautiful, my wife, and I could only be described as handsome in my dreams. The woman in the SUV is lit perfectly as she steers the vehicle away from the helicopter and heads over the side of the skyscraper. Behind her head, clouds are passing blithely over the Manhattan skyline, the clouds shaped in oddly sexual contours, fleecy, bouncy, and white as my laundry when I add the proper additives and use the most expensive front-loading washer. This wife has perfect, glistening lips and glossy, even teeth. I hardly remember what the husband looks like from the front, though his rear-end clenches, first one side, then the other, as he climbs into the helicopter. My backside no longer has any clench to speak of, and I would be wise to answer the next penis enlargement advertisement that enters unbidden into my email inbox. I may hire a personal trainer, perhaps Jake himself. After my crime spree I expect my personal ratings to soar, in terms of attention, and I want to be camera-shiny.

For instance, Katie Couric will ignore my divorce but when I murder my wife in some spectacular fashion, Katie will have me on the *Today* show or *Dateline*. I prefer Katie Couric and Barbara Walters to all the rest. Diane Sawyer on *Good Morning America* is a pretty close third. As for Jane Pauley, I hold her in too much awe, I would be tongue-tied in her presence. When I found out she was bipolar I went to bed for a week. Anyway, for the interview, Katie and I will walk along a path in the autumn woods, the same path as when she interviewed pixie-pretty little Elizabeth Smart, fresh home from her abduction. Leaves will drift down in various colors through the clear, beautiful day, me in a comfortable cardigan, something between blue and gray, a soft tone that won't compete with the rich colors of the leaves or the bright blue of the sky. Katie will ask, same as she asked Elizabeth, "Did this change your life?"

"Yes," I'll say. "I'm sorry my wife had to die, but the house is quieter. I sleep better with both sides of the bed set to my personal sleep number. And I don't have to worry about whether she will share her box of Cheez-Its with me." By then I will have many sponsors, I will need to use my opportunities to do aggressive product placement, but I'll have a team of assistants, like a hip-hop star; I'll have an entourage, including armed bodyguards, though none of them will be visible in the edited interview as it is broadcast, first in abbreviated fashion during the seven a.m. segment of *Today* and later, the full twenty minute version on *Dateline*, the Sunday night edition, when most people are at home.

"Are you ever sorry for what you did?" she'll ask.

I won't know how to answer. I'll gaze thoughtfully into the drifting leaves, pensive, moody, lit through gauze.

Our cars can do the most wonderful things. Driving up a building is only the beginning. Our vehicles gleam, soar down lonely roads between verdant fields, hug the curve of a mountain as tightly as a lover, plow through streams of water, conquer boulders, park on the sides of cliffs, appear in the vast icy wasteland of the arctic; our cars are superheroes in the making, with driver-side airbags, passenger airbags, side curtain airbags, anti-lock braking systems, LoJack theft recovery system, satellite positioning, moonroofs; my wife wants a new Mercedes SUV but I am out of work, our money nearly gone, and now she asks for a divorce. Is it because I can't buy her a new car or make love to her or both?

I have fallen in love with another woman, a slender part-Asian with thick eyebrows who wears her hair pulled back in a ponytail, loose and supple; I've never met her but I've seen her on television, on a commercial, marvelously lit, including the elegant floor lighting that made shows like X-*Files* so remarkable, floods of light pouring towards her from all directions. In the commercial she has a Caucasian husband in a white shirt and tie with a pen in his pocket. His tie is striped on a slant rising from the left to right as I view him, and including four colors of stripe: black, grey, mauve, and turquoise. The first time I saw the commercial I thought it was for the car but later I realized it was a cell phone commercial. The Asian woman was sitting in an SUV beside her handsome husband, but what she was trying to sell me was her silence, rather than the SUV. Her husband was better looking than me but he could have been me if I still worked out. She was sitting beside him looking away, into the distance, into the clouds, silent. She and her husband have been arguing, and she and I have that in common, that we have been arguing with our spouses. Later this couple makes up by sending text messages over their cell phones when they are each in a meeting, another kind of silence; but at the moment in which I fell in love with her, she was angry with him, her mate, both of them still in the car, and he sat there puzzled but inert, looking with some confusion ahead, driving handsomely and safely forward, troubled about his relations with this attractive woman who could have been my woman, in that car that could have been my car.

"You're gay," says my wife, Lauren. She is of that generation in which nearly all the girls were named Lauren, sometimes spelled in variants like Lauryn, Laurin, Loran, or Lah Rynne. For this reason she now goes by her middle name, Carmine, which was her grandmother's name. She currently has brown hair and has always had brown eyes. Her skin is stretched by facelifts and deadened by Botox. Her chin is dimpled but still gives the impression of being pointed. No matter what kind of hair style she chooses, she has a bouncy look, which has grown more pronounced as she ages and becomes more ample.

"What are you talking about? I'm not gay. You just accused me of having an affair with a woman."

"You told me you were gay." She makes a gesture as if she

is waving a cigarette at me, a Benson & Hedges, long and slim, the way she used to when she smoked. She quit smoking but kept the gesture. "When you were drunk. You told me you slept with my brother. Or he told me. That's another reason I want a divorce."

She makes up these stories because she knows I don't remember what happens when I'm drunk. Vodka is my drink these days. When we were in school together our liquor was tequila. In our early-to-middle married years I drank gin. But to accuse me of having sex with her brother, even drunk, is outrageous, as if anyone would sleep with bony Edgar with his ghoulish face. If I were gay, I still wouldn't sleep with her brother, but I'm not. I shake my head. "You know I'm not gay. Who would want your brother? He has bad breath."

I have a flash of myself killing her, vaguely, as if my hands would like to reach for her throat on their own; only vaguely, only the shadow of it, this first time, but I can feel how real it is. When she looks at me, she has no idea. She waves her hand at me. "You're a crook and a cheat and a slut," she says. "You would screw anything that would lay there for it."

We are standing in the breakfast area, what I once called a breakfast nook only to have Carmine give me her most withering look. It is a week now since she told me she wants a divorce. I am near the round greystone table scattered with opened jars of marmalade and Polaner All Fruit, half-eaten bagels and English muffins on white china plates, light falling from the bay window, or bow window, as Carmine prefers to call it. I am about to head to the local Starbucks to read the national edition of the *New York Times*; I prefer to read the newspaper at a coffee shop because it gives me more of a sense of having an occupation. We are long past the point where we pretend that I am leaving the house every morning on a diligent search for a new job. The only one likely to be looking for work in our house these days is Carmine, and her threats to launch her own imminent career as a something-or-other are a sure sign that our marriage is near its last gasp. She has not held a job since the first year we were married, a very long time ago. She's thinking she can sell clothes in the local Bloomingdale's or Neiman Marcus, a wise choice, since she herself has spent a fortune at both stores and knows their merchandise thoroughly. So far, of course, even Carmine's hunt for employment is mostly theoretical.

Her eyes mist a bit and she looks at me with a moment's softness as she begins to clear the remains of her breakfast from the table. I am no longer allowed to take my meals with her, so none of this food waste is mine. "Charley," she says, "what happened to you? You were such a good man."

The question galls me; a more appropriate question might be, "What happened to us?" or, "What happened to our love for one another?" Even in a moment of slightly reminiscent tenderness, like this one, Carmine is angling for position, claiming the political high ground for our upcoming legal separation. The story will be how Charley changed, not how Charley and Carmine failed one another. I can feel myself shivering with renewed anger, my hands trembling to touch her throat again, and so I quickly turn on my heel and head for the door. I have the car keys in my pocket, the weight bouncing against my thigh. On the kitchen television is another commercial with a Polynesian woman washing her lustrous dark hair and gazing seductively up a flow of water into the camera. She is not my true love but she reminds me of my true love. The effect is shocking, as if I have walked into that fall of clear, cold water myself.

I find I have stopped dead in my tracks. This kitchen television is one of the new Sony plasma screens, the picture crisp as a still photograph, assembling and reassembling itself in front of my eyes millions of times and ways each second, and all that motion adds up in my pre-frontal cortex to this image of a smooth, polished, beautiful woman who has an air of unshakeable serenity, an assurance of eternal calm, and lustrous, supple waves of hair. When I turn to my wife she is standing in the middle of the kitchen with a piece of bagel in her hand, the remains of last week's spray tan beginning to fade, her eyes lighter than the rest of her skin, and a pale edge around her face from the bathing cap she wears when the tan sprayer lathers her with this fake color; she looks like a Malibu raccoon. Her housecoat, which she calls a morning robe, falls sheer and simple around her Victoria's Secret nightgown. Underneath this is her body, for which breast implants, liposuction, a tummy tuck, and various other grades of adjustments have failed to stave off the coming of middle age. She looks worse than old; she looks like a failed medical experiment, ghastly even at the beginning of her decay.

"I'll tell you what happened to us," I say. "Look at you. Look at you there. How much money did we spend on that carcass of yours?"

She blinks, mildly energized by the fact that I am still in the room, that I have not taken the occasion of her moment of nostalgia to flee. "What are you talking about?"

"Tell me how much it all adds up to. We had your breasts enlarged because they were the size of peach pits. Then we had them reduced because you got them too big the first time and you had a backache. We had the fat sucked out of your ass how many times? Once a year was it? We had your nose trimmed, even though your daddy gave you a nose job for your high school graduation. We got you so many high colonics I could have bought my own irrigation system. What else? The face lift? The attempt to make your ass look a little less like a landslide? How much does it all add up to?"

Forgiveness 7

A color, a genuine, natural color, is rising up her throat and crossing her cheeks. "What kind of crap are you trying to start here, Charley?"

"I'm asking a simple question. How much money have we spent on your fucking ugliness? A hundred thousand? Two? I'm not even talking about the wardrobe, the jewelry, the shoes, none of that crap. I'm not even talking about the house. How much money have we flushed down the toilet of this disaster you call your body? How much?"

"You don't even want to go there," she says.

"Your teeth could use whitening," I say. "They're as yellow as summer squash."

"Fuck you," she says.

"Maybe another face lift, too," I say. "Then maybe your pubic hair would reach all the way to your chin and you could wear a beard."

"I don't believe my ears," she says. "This comedy from the man whose body shape approximates one of the Teletubbies. One of the fucking Teletubbies," and here she's speaking so forcefully that she spits a bit, a fleck of saliva on her chin. "The purple one, the gay one."

"Maybe we need to get radical," I continue, ignoring the spit, "maybe instead of liposuction we just need to ask Dr. Brewski to carve off big chunks of you at the waist."

"His name is not Brewski. It's Brynowski. And you know that perfectly well, you limpid mother-fucker, you cheese dick."

"You talk like the gutter-mouth you are," I say. "Like that slob of a mother of yours. Is she awake yet? You think she's listening?"

"You leave my mother out of this."

"Your mother is in this up to her pruny ass, Carmine. Your mother is in this up to her rheumy eyeballs."

"Listen to you with your big vocabulary."

"You'd prefer I stuck to the four letter words like you do, I guess. Get your mother out here right now, let's have a look at the two of you together. Mother and daughter, surgical miracles."

"Get out of here, Charley." She's trembling, moving to the sink, shoving the last chunk of bagel into the garbage disposal.

"Don't waste that bagel," I say, "not after you slathered a pound of butter and cream cheese and fruit gunk all over it. Think of the starving people in Rio de Janeiro. Think of the poor Africans. Don't waste that bagel, shove it down your throat."

Something comes whizzing past my head to fall behind me in the kitchen. There's no sound of breakage, it's not the china, Carmine is too canny for real destruction. Probably the sponge from the sink, the one she leaves there to wipe up spills between visits from the Serbian maid. Carmine is breathing like she wants to heave a fireball at me, as if she is truly the dragon that I sometimes accuse her of being. "You need to get out of this kitchen, right now," she says.

"Why? You want to pick up a knife and throw it at me next?"

"Get out, Charley. Before I do something I won't like."

I chuckle. "Let me just stand here and imagine what that might be."

"You no-good out-of-work son-of-a-bitch."

"Throw that in my face," I say, "who cares? You've been out of work for twenty-five years, right? But that's all right. You can sit here on your I-wish-I-could-get-a-butt-implant-so-I-could-look-like-J-Lo ass for twenty-five years, a quarter of a century, and that's okay; you can suck up every dime I earned into this rotting carcass you walk around in, and that's okay; but let me be out of work for a few stinking months and what do I hear?"

"A few stinking months? Charley, it's been three years."

"You're a liar. You want a divorce? Well let me tell you something, dearie sweetheart, mother of my children. I'll give you a divorce. I'll give you a whole pile of divorce like a big stinking dump-truck load of feces. Do you hear me? Do you?"

But I don't wait to find out. With an exit line like that one, it is irresistible to storm out of the house, and so I do, out the door next to the utility room, down the brick steps into the carport and trotting toward my car, lighter than I've felt in days.

IN THE LIFETIME CHANNEL movie version of Carmine's divorce, that scene will play a good deal differently. Carmine will be played by Virginia Madsen or Courteney Cox-Arquette, or, at worst, by Kirstie Alley, plump but voluptuous. I will be played by someone far less well-known, someone like Tom Arnold, but less recognizable. Carmine's dialogue will be rewritten to exclude the gutter language, and her appearance, standing in the kitchen, will be skillfully manipulated to invite more sympathy. I'll look pretty much like myself, I expect, a pudgy slob in expensive slacks and shoes, neatly shaven but not as well washed as I used to be, in the days when I still showered every morning before heading to my job at Arthur Andersen.

In the movie, just before our big scene in the kitchen, there'll be shots of Carmine reading our love letters from after college, when I was working as an administrative intern for a hospital in Milwaukee and she was finishing her senior year at Georgia Tech. She'll be reading the letter I wrote where I called her my tiny goddess of love, or something like that; she read that letter over and over again the year she was pregnant with Ann, because it had touched her so much, she said. Carmine/Virginia in the movie will read the letter with tears welling in her eyes, the classic movie shot: she finds the letter, recognizes it, and sinks slowly onto the bed, framed by a beautifully lit window; Carmine/Virginia will let the letter fall into her lap, sobs rising in her throat, wondering, so obviously, how she and I came to this pass, a more generous version of the question she asked me in the kitchen. In the Lifetime Channel movie, entitled *Tender Is the Dawn*, the divorce will be Carmine's divorce, and I will play the part of the villain. This is all right with me, since this is the role I've decided to take on myself, anyway.

Will she be afraid for her life? When we know a murder is coming, foreshadowing appears all around us, at least on TV. In real life, right now, Carmine is thinking about other things: how to find a divorce lawyer, how to convince me to move out of the house peaceably, how to explain to Ann and Frank that their parents are splitting up, how to make it look like it's not the fact that I'm out of work that's pissed her off, that she's not abandoning me so that she can take the house and the bank account for herself, while there's still something left.

She thinks there's something left, anyway. She has a rude awakening coming, next time she uses her ATM card.

The fact that I'm thinking about ways to kill her is hardly likely to be on her mind, because a thought like that is so out of character for me. It's the last thing Carmine will suspect. But in the movie, through clever use of foreshadowing, the audience will see it coming.

The Lifetime movie told from my point of view, my version of my divorce and crime spree, will be entitled *Breakdown at Midnight*. I will still play the part of the bad guy, but my character will get more screen time, and I will be played by a handsome leading actor like Dean Cain or Antonio Sabato, Jr. I will play the typical sadistic, uncaring, belligerent, philandering, extremely attractive husband. Maybe this will be one of the more daring movies and my lover, the one Carmine is certain I have, will actually be a man, or will even be her brother. Sympathy for my character will be established by my loss of a wildly respectable, lucrative job with Arthur Andersen, a company which turned out to be as crooked as its customers. I will be another orphan of the American Dream gone sour, and eventually I will give in to the so-called dark side of my nature when I strangle Carmine with the strap of her Prada bag, or stab her to death with a survivalist-quality hunting knife, or bludgeon her skull to a bloody pulp with a classic Tiffany lamp; this part of the script will have to wait for the real event to unfold since, though I've decided that tomorrow will be the day I kill her, I have yet to choose how.

An Ordinary Person, Much Like Yourself

I DRIVE TO A STARBUCKS for my morning latte. The clerk at the Starbucks is a dead ringer for Queen Latifah, but perhaps not as physically fit, since this young woman looks a bit like two hundred pounds of dark cheese poured into spandex pants and a black knit shirt, covered by a Starbucks green apron. At this Starbucks, the employees wear plastic name tags. Her name tag reads, "Teefallah," and she has three gold earrings in one ear, six in the other, a gold stud through one nostril, and one bright gold tooth right in front.

"What can I get for you?" she asks, the gold tooth gleaming.

"Double shot latte with whole milk," I say. "How are you?"

"I'm all jiggly with it," she says, or something that sounds like that, and her co-worker, a thin Latina with a nervous smile, gives her a sidelong look. "I love this good weather."

I smile and act as if I know exactly what she just said. "You move up here from Miami?" I ask, because of the tooth.

She creases her eyebrows together, suspicious. "No, sweetie, I didn't move here from anywhere." She drops change from my five-dollar bill into my palm, her long, multicolored nails adorned with cut-outs, stars, and patches of glitter. "What's in Miami, anyway?"

I carry my cup to one of the polished, round tables by the window, on which someone has conveniently left a discarded copy of today's *Times*.

There is something about the décor of a Starbucks that makes me feel comfortable, yet up-to-the-minute. This particular Starbucks is always teeming with customers. I'm reading the *New York Times* Bestseller List in the Book Review when a woman in dark glasses asks if she can join me at my table. By this time the rest of the tables are full. She slides into her seat with her cup. The woman wears a mauve scarf, very simple, but obviously expensive, over a finely woven sweater-blouse that looks even more chic than Carmine's best designer items. Designer scent washes over me. The woman removes the scarf and shakes out strawberry blonde hair, abundant as a waterfall, shimmering like a shampoo commercial, and, judging by the luster of her hair and her pearl-white, perfect skin, I recognize her as N— K—, the famous movie actress and Oscar winner.

I'm stunned by the fact that she's here, that she's sat down with me. She removes her sunglasses with a knowing glance in my direction, realizing at once that I have recognized her and that I am much too sophisticated to say so. She pinches off a morsel of her cranberry muffin and slips it into her bare, soft lips. Not a shred of makeup on that flawless skin.

We sit in silence, each sipping our coffee, and I offer her part of my *Times*; to my surprise she asks for the sports section, and I detect the slight lilt of her Australian accent as she thanks me. She reads quietly, her lips forming the most perfect touch of a pout as she does.

After a while, N— says to me, in an undertone, glancing around, "This place is awfully busy this morning, for a weekday."

"It's getting to be too popular," I say. "I may have to start driving farther out of town."

She nods demurely, sliding more muffin into that prime, kissable mouth of hers. She gives me a kind of come-on look; her face, it appears, has been frozen into a series of come-on expressions, each as artful and subtle as the last, and therefore I do not feel any sexual excitement or have any notion that she is purposefully cruising me. She has that quality that all fine actors and actresses have, of being able to see herself from all angles at once, of constantly watching herself. When I glance from my newspaper to her perfectly composed face, I feel as if I have become not a would-be suitor but a blissful movie camera, recording each spark of light from her cheekbones, searching for any marks left by that fake nose she wore when she played Virginia Woolf in *The Hours*. Not a mark, not a line, not a flaw. "I've seen you in here before," she says.

She enjoys my surprise. I had no idea she was a regular in this neighborhood. "It's a little out of my way, but I like the drive," I answer. "Gives me time to think."

"You sound like a man who has a lot to think about."

"It's nothing," I say modestly. "A few problems at home."

"We all have those." She's looking outside now, into the perfect blue of the sky, the swell of the Pacific waves; I think maybe she's checking the parking lot for paparazzi, though I've never seen a single photographer here, no matter what famous person has dropped in for a cup of coffee-of-the-day. "Anything serious?"

"My wife has asked me for a divorce." I shrug. "And I'm out of a job. The usual."

Her eyes flood with a moist sympathy that gives me goose pimples on my forearms. "Poor you," she says, and injects the whole of her soul into the words.

"Nothing I can't handle." I'm getting a bit of an erection, so I cross my legs.

"You know I've had the same problem, of course."

"I knew about your divorce. Not that I was going to ask any questions. You know. About your ex-husband."

She nods with perfect grace. "It's not just the divorce that you and I have in common, either," she says. "Actors are constantly out of work. So I have nothing but empathy for you there, too."

"Thank you."

"You do seem to be holding up well."

I lean forward in a conspiratorial way. "Can I ask you a personal question?" Hurriedly completing the thought before she gets the wrong impression. "Not about . . . him, or about your marriage, or, God help us, your children. About your emotions."

As she smiles, a gray-and-white gull dips into the air above the parking lot behind her head, hanging, wings spread, in that eerie way that gulls have, and for a moment she wears it as a hat. She has become Tippi Hedren in *The Birds*. "I don't mind."

"Did you ever have violent feelings? I mean, a longing to do something violent. When you and . . . he . . . broke up?"

"I should say. I wanted to rip his heart out. Well, not actually his heart." She shudders at the memory, as deliciously as if some camera is recording this moment.

"That's a relief," I say.

"What about you?"

"I can't deny that I've had thoughts."

She's watching me carefully, as if she's studying me for some part she's working on, some mannerism or facial tic that she finds interesting. "You can't blame yourself for that."

"My wife claims she thinks I'm gay."

"Claims?" She arches one perfectly shaped eyebrow.

"I don't think she's serious. This is a psychological war, and she's trying to win any way she can."

"You don't think she's serious?"

"Well," I say, adjusting my belt buckle a bit, sunken beneath my overhanging gut, "I'm not gay, if that's what you mean."

She is studying the beautiful manicure of her nails. "I'm sure you're not."

She's thinking about T— her ex-husband, I'm sure. I ask, "Did you ever want to hurt him?"

Her eyes have suddenly grown very sad. "We were very happy. At one time."

"But that didn't keep you from having violent thoughts?"

She shakes her head. From the table she lifts her sunglasses as if she'd like to put them on again. "What about you, what's your fantasy? What do you want to do to your wife?"

I lower my eyes. "I'd better not tell you what I have in mind." My whisper is conspiratorial, and draws her closer to the table.

"Why not?"

"Better that you don't know. In case the police find out we've talked." I sit up straight, look her in the eye. "I wouldn't want you implicated."

"Oh." She sits back and blinks and understands. It is as if

a curtain has gone down between us. She waits a moment longer before standing; she's wearing the most perfect, form-fitting pair of jeans I've ever seen, and no belt at all. "It's been so wonderful to talk to you," she says. "I do hope we run into each other again."

"Maybe we will," I say, though my heart is pounding as I watch the sunglasses travel so gracefully to cover her eyes. "I come here rather often."

At some point during our conversation she has put on lipstick, a glistening, wet, expensive pink. She walks away as if we had never been talking. She's afraid of me now, she knows that I'm planning something terrible. Tomorrow, I remind myself, as N— ties the scarf over her shining hair and disappears into the parking lot, carrying what's left of her mocha. Tomorrow this will all be over. Even a major star like N— K— can't stop me in that short space of time.

You Always Kill the One You Love

THERE ARE TWO KINDS of people in America: those who want publicity and can't get it, and those who attract too much publicity and can't escape it.

The question, in my case, is no longer whether I will kill my wife, but how will I do it in a way that guarantees me maximum attention from the press.

Certain kinds of murderers have advantages that I will never share. A killer with a Heisman Trophy, for instance, begins his crime spree with a ready-made notoriety and a financial war chest that will be difficult for a non-athlete like me to duplicate.

Other famous killings are impossible to imitate for various reasons. Much as I hate Carmine at the moment, I could hardly, for instance, drown her in the waters of the

San Francisco Bay, or any other bay, for that matter. Over the years of our marriage, Carmine has consistently refused any contact with large bodies of water; she prefers mountains (in which she does not hike), ski resorts (at which she does not ski), or large hotels in inland cities (in which she orders room service and rests between shopping trips). To this tenacious disinclination she has clung in spite of the fact that many bodies of water are the haunts of fashionable and expensive friends of ours, which makes me believe this aversion to be all the more genuine. She has, in fact, what I would call a morbid fear of any volume of water greater than the pool in our back yard, in which, of course, she does not swim. So this rules out any death similar to those visited on Laci Peterson or Natalie Wood. Though I am reminded, of course, that Laci most likely did not drown but was already dead when she went into the water.

I am a fairly weak swimmer myself, and would have to admit, though only under duress, that it has been quite some time since I viewed our pool as anything more than an interesting art object, a water installation, and that I have no emptiness in my life that would be filled by walks along the sandy tides. I would not wish to be seen as presuming any moral superiority over my wife, as if that could justify what I am about to do.

Other varieties of spousal murder, or the murder of significant others, are interesting but unlikely, as the case of Julia Lynn Womack Turner who was indicted for poisoning her police officer husband by tricking him into drinking antifreeze. A later boyfriend, a firefighter, also died by ingesting engine coolant under mysterious circumstances, before Lynn was brought before the courts and the cameras. Perhaps, if she had not been caught, she would have married a soldier next, or a member of the Georgia State Patrol, or a forest ranger, completing a whole set of murdered public servants. Death by ethylene glycol mimics natural death by an irregular heartbeat, leaving little evidence, and even tastes sweet, making it perhaps the perfect choice for a fellow with a hearty sweet tooth. However, my Carmine has highly developed taste buds and a very sensitive palate, as any number of local and area restaurant waiters will attest; short of pouring the fluid down her throat while she is sleeping, I consider it to be unlikely that I will be able, for instance, to trick her into drinking special homemade punch.

The kind of murder I have in mind is of a peculiar character, since it must earn for me all the bounty of fame and celebrity without the appearance of seeking to do so. I prefer to be seen as other than grasping; I prefer to sit, Womack-like, perfectly composed in the courthouse, dressed in neat pantsuits with my electronic detection anklet discretely concealed, my eyes spaced perhaps less widely than hers, in order to appear more photogenic than demented. I owe Carmine that much, not to make a mockery of her death.

For other reasons, a simple contract killing appears out of the question. First of all, in order for me to achieve any kind of real publicity, my part in the murder must inevitably be found out. A contract killer might prove to be too efficient, or, if detected, too mundane. Anyone with a little money can pay to have his wife, or her husband, killed; there's no originality or verve in it; I could probably make the arrangements online if I were willing to risk sending my credit card information over the internet.

The most expedient solution to the dilemma would be to murder others at the same time as Carmine, as an expression of rage, perhaps because of my many months of unemployment. Were my children still of a tender age, I might stab their mother to death and then slit their throats, preferably at some wee hour of the morning with Frank in his footed pajamas and Annette nestled in a cotton nightie. I suppose, given the power and convenience of the automobile, that I could drive to X and attack Frank in his comfortable house, and then buzz over to that little town in Y to do the same to Annette and her skinny girlfriend. Slaughtering in three states would certainly do me justice in terms of exposure. But there's the inconvenience, the added risk of capture, not to mention triple the clean-up.

Carmine deserves an original end. She has been, at times, a good mate, probably better than I have been. She deserves the best, the most creative, murder that I can contrive. Not some cheap passion killing but a true piece of planning and art. She deserves my all.

For Carmine, I must do better than the cheap, lurid spectacle of massacre performed by Mark O. Barton, the Atlanta day trader who shot his wife Leigh Ann, his two children Matthew and Mychelle, and nine people in two Buckhead stock brokerage offices; and who very likely killed his first wife, Debra, years before. While his motives may have sprung from the same roots as my own, though both Mark O. Barton and I have lost fabulous sums of money in the stock market and have in general presided over the financial ruin of our families, I myself don't have the sort of self-satisfied self-preoccupation that would allow me to bother so many of my neighbors and fellow beings in that way. I can understand his wanting to shoot and kill his family, an impulse familiar to anyone who has ever been a member of a family, and certainly can sympathize with his shooting the second wife if he had already gotten away with killing the first. It's certain that this kind of killing spree would guarantee me the public exposure usually reserved for rock stars and movie idols, which is, of course, what I seek. But it would be a false and immoral way of murdering my faithful Carmine, who deserves that her death should not be diluted in gallons of blood from other people. Besides, I would have to shoot myself at the end of the killing spree, and I doubt I'd ever muster the nerve for that.

I think Carmine would very much prefer to be stabbed than to be shot. If she were choosing the manner of her death, or, to be more specific, if she were choosing a method by which she would be murdered, I expect she would opt for poison, perhaps a quick-acting overdose of sleeping pills, if any such dosage exists. But as I have said, there is the problem that Carmine is instinctively and totally persnickety about what she eats, along with an occasional difficulty in swallowing at all, and almost certainly would be suspicious of any sudden interest I might evince in preparing our dinner or bringing her a spontaneous snack.

Perhaps I could slip some sort of toxin in her Gatorade, which she persists in drinking as if she were a teenage athlete shedding buckets of sweat. How much antifreeze would it take to make a liter of Gatorade into a lethal potion? Perhaps if I had made it all the way through two terms of Organic Chemistry in college, I might have the proper tools for calculating this; but I ran screaming from a pre-med curriculum to the business school as fast as my plump legs would carry me. On the other hand, I could simply type "Julia Lynn Womack Turner" into Google and see what proportion of the cocktail she used.

How much research am I prepared to do? Is there a fatal dosage of Ambien, and, if the answer is yes, might Carmine already be approaching it on her own? How about that little purple pill she takes for depression, or the one she takes to improve her sex drive, that strikes terror into the heart of her poor abused vibrator? Is it possible to make some deadly combination out of her current stock of prescription and non-prescription medications? Could I induce diabetes in some way, and then inject her with too much insulin, like a simple von Bulow?

If Carmine dies simply and quickly, that will never be enough to get me in all the blogs. What exactly do I have to do?

What's my hurry? Why rush toward murder in such a bee-line; why tomorrow? I have my reasons. The most pressing is self-preservation. Though it's true that most often a husband kills his wife, at least forty percent of the time it's the wife who kills the husband. I've done a certain amount of poking about in statistics, you see. While I plan a fitting end to Carmine's existence, she may very well be doing the same for mine.

Not the Thing Itself but the Appearance of the Thing

WHEN I DRIVE HOME from the Starbucks, Carmine's Lexus is out of the driveway, but there's a silver Honda Accord, about six years old, that I recognize as belonging to the twice-a-week maid, a Serb named Deutze. Today I have vowed to tell Deutze that this is her last week, that I don't have any more money to pay her, but as soon as I see her car my resolve vanishes, and a fear of my own poverty strikes me cold in the heart. Deutze is in the kitchen scrubbing all the stainless steel surfaces with a toothbrush. She is on her hands and knees at the moment, her bulbous hips thrust upward, working furiously at cleaning the bottom of the oven door, propped on one arm and scrubbing with the other, studying the stainless steel intently as she works it over. The angle of her knees and the way her whole chunky weight presses onto her kneecaps makes me wince.

My knees crack and pop with every step I take. She looks back at me, and for the second time I think she's had a shot of collagen in her lips; she looks like what might happen if someone grafted Angelina Jolie's mouth onto the face of Dustin Hoffman as Tootsie. Her ample rump is jiggling as she scrubs, and she never stops scrubbing, even when she glares at me in that come-hither way of hers. If only I were a cheating man, I would grapple her into the bedroom right now and show her what a force of nature I can be. For a moment I entertain the fantasy. But in reality I am only a little squall in the stormy ocean of love, and Deutze, whom I believe to be aggressively experienced, turns away from me in contempt.

She has already cleaned the dining room and pulled the drapes closed. We have a wide window in that room that looks onto the garden at the side of the house, where there's a fountain and a replica of that statue from the cover of *Midnight in the Garden of Good and Evil*, Carmine's favorite book. At the moment the garden is obscured behind the custom-made drapes at the window, densely pleated, some shade between white-beige and white-gray. A week ago in this room Carmine asked me for a divorce. I spent the next three days drunk in the pool house.

At first, when she said the words, I could hardly believe my ears. "What are you talking about? What's wrong with you?"

"There's nothing wrong with me," she said. "I can't watch you do this to yourself, that's all."

"Do what to myself?"

"Ruin yourself. Sit around for the rest of your life."

"I'm not going to sit around for the rest of my life. I'm going to get another job."

"Charley, it's been three years already. You think I'm believing this crap that you're still looking for a job?"

"It's only been six months."

"Six months since you got fired from that real estate company. You can't even sell real estate."

"I still had a job. It still counts. You know damn well it hasn't been three years."

"Please, Charley, why would I lie about that? Why would I make that up?"

"There are some great leads today on the internet," I say. "Deloitte and Touche is hiring. They have a lot of my old clients."

She made that blowing sound with her mouth; she's not quite as good at it since she started having her lips done more often, since the Botox. A fleck of spit flew out and arced across the dining table. "Come on. Who are you kidding?"

"I'm telling the truth about Deloitte and Touche. And they're not the only place. I'm online every day, checking what's out there. I mailed out a hundred resumes since the real estate place. More than a hundred."

"How many times do I have to say it? All your friends from Arthur Andersen got jobs. Every one. Except you. Can you explain that, Mr. I-Look-For-A-Job-Every-Day? Can you?"

I glared at her. She was telling the truth. A change of subject was in order. "You're divorcing me because I can't find a job?"

"I'm divorcing you because you're not even looking for a job."

I turned slowly in the room, hands out, gesturing to the house and everything in it. "Tell me what I'm missing here. We live in a great house. You have everything you want. What am I doing wrong?"

"We're spending every cent we have. You're almost broke. You think I don't know it but I do. I'm getting out while I still can." When I started to talk she waved her arms at me, not even the hint of a tear in her eye, all business. "That's enough. I've listened to you enough. I'm not listening any more. We're getting a divorce." She flapped her hands out from the fingertips, showing that expensive French manicure; this gesture is a sign of complete dismissal, and after she gave it, she walked out of the room.

In this room. She lacked the decency to end our marriage in our bedroom, which might have shown an ounce of consideration for my feelings. She gave me the news right here in the dining room over the nearly-new Mission dining table that seats sixteen. Absent the least hint of regret.

Today, a week later, I am standing in front of those expensive drapes wishing I were the kind of boss who could throw Deutze over a couch and show her the manly stuff I'm made of, or at least demand that she fix me a drink. But I can't even bring myself to tell her I can't afford a maid any more.

My confidence as a sexual partner has been destroyed by a constant bombardment of penis enlargement ads in my email inbox, sent by a conspiracy of persons who wish to reinforce my feelings of inadequacy. I have been tempted by such products as MagnaX and TriplThik, I have come close to spraying one of my credit card numbers perilously over the internet; I have come close to risking what remains of my self-respect by allowing an electronic audit trail to exist that will verify for anyone who cares that I think my penis is too small.

This is more of a fear than a thought. But it persists.

My penis is certainly tiny most of the time. Gone are the days when it could rage and stiffen like a bull; but, alas for me, those days were mostly gone by the time I switched from hand to girl.

I only ever had sex with three girls, Carmine, and Betsy, and Caroline. Since I didn't marry Betsy or Caroline I don't see any reason to talk about them except to say that Betsy was high school and Caroline was freshman year in college and neither of them was evidence of much ardor on my part since our sex was jerky and quick and immensely infrequent.

When Carmine and I did make love, in the days after our marriage got settled, Carmine would fake her orgasms, wait for me to fall asleep, and finish herself in the bathroom with her vibrator, an awesome instrument that left me with deep feelings of unease when I heard its steady thrum. I waited up one night and heard the battery powered friend slide out of the drawer of the bedside table, saw her swing it jauntily as she crossed to the bathroom and closed the door. She came back to bed a few minutes later, sighing. After that whenever we had sex I quickly pretended to fall asleep and listened to her use the vibrator in the bathroom.

My own orgasms took on a tentative quality, and I started faking them, too, after a while. She must have noticed, since there was no longer any messy product of any kind, but she was too kind a woman to mention this, until recently.

Pretty soon I was having my only real sex with my hand again, and my wife was stocking batteries by the carton.

Once in a while we would shock each other, though, like that time in her mother's house the night her father died when we shook the bed against the walls so hard her mother came and knocked on the door. Once in a while it was fine to be under and on top of and around her, and we felt like partners and equals and we got a little lost in each other. Like in college, in the first days when we started having sex, but better, because now we knew each other.

Even at the worst moments, we never stopped pretending to have sex with each other, which was a sign that we cared for each other, wasn't it?

A year ago, after we hired Deutze, my wife cornered me in

the bedroom with her eyes bulging and jammed her index finger into my collarbone. "I know you've been fucking this East European piece of shit, Charley. Admit it."

"Admit what? Deutze? Are you out of your mind, she'd kill me if I laid a hand on her."

"Oh, you coward. You can't even tell the truth when I confront you."

"Lauren, what on earth can you be thinking, what can possibly be in your brain? Have you seen the thighs on that woman? She would crack me like a matchstick."

She shoved me backwards onto the bed and climbed on top of me, squeezing me with her own thighs. "Don't call me Lauren. That's not my name."

"Carmine, then. What are you doing?"

"Showing you what my thighs can do," she said, and squeezed the breath out of me, meanwhile rubbing against me. Both our bodies were ample and soft along the front, comfortable and wieldy.

"Deutze is here," I said, "she'll hear."

"Your whore Deutze," she said. "You're worried your whore might hear you fuck your wife?"

"Carmine, please, I never touched her."

"Shut up, you stupid little worm."

She accused me to bolster my ego, to say she wanted me again. Maybe she played the vixen that day because it was on her mind to reward me. I was trying to sell real estate at the time, and she wanted me to know she was grateful. We made a valiant attempt at fancy foreplay and I mounted her almost like a stud. But I suspect in the end she was disappointed.

Maybe NaturalGain+ is the product I really need. Three more inches of myself and it would be harder for her to turn to Mr. Plastic. Three more inches and certainly, surely, I would feel more aroused myself.

This talk of her brother is to punish me and recurs from time to time. I think Edgar actually told her this story years ago, that I went to bed with him one night when we were both drunk. It would be like him; a man so brazen he covers the bathroom of his house with pictures of naked men making love to each other, with no shame or feeling of degradation, from every conceivable position and some, indeed, that I never would have conceived had I not seen them.

The reason I think he's told her this story is very simple. He talked to me about this incident the day after it allegedly happened. Carmine was in the hospital undergoing expensive problems with her pregnancy, similar to the problems that some of our more sensitive neighbors were having, including a bit of blood spotting that was real enough to make the doctors put her on her back. Edgar came to visit her in the hospital and stayed in our guest room. One night, as he claimed, we had dinner, drank a lot of wine, and went to bed together.

"Then why did I wake up in my own bed?" I asked.

"You got up and left about dawn. You were probably still drunk. You were really loaded."

"Loaded or not, I think I would remember having sex with you, Edgar."

"Lord, Charley, you never remember anything when you're really drunk."

"I'd remember that."

"Why?"

"I've never had sex with a man before."

Edgar gave me a look.

"I haven't," I said.

"Well, you sure knew what to do."

"Edgar, we didn't do anything."

"Don't worry. I won't tell Carmine."

Which was, of course, a rank lie.

"There's nothing to tell her."

"Of course there's not." He looked smug, and sauntered to a window, with something of the air of Bette Davis before the cocktail party in *All About Eve*. The nerve of the man. As if my gay debut, should there ever be one, would find me paired with someone so angular and scrawny.

"Come on, Ed, I know when I've had sex or not. I can tell."

"How?"

"I can just tell. My penis feels used."

"Used?"

"Yes." I set my jaw and stood as he started to grin.

"Well, it felt pretty used last night," he said. Which was what I might have expected.

"You flatter yourself."

"What?"

I decided there was no need to be nice. "I would never have sex with you, Ed. You are the last man on earth I would have sex with."

"Because of Lauren. Carmine."

We were all still getting used to the new name. "No. Because you're ugly. Because you're not my type."

His face set into an unpleasant expression and he reached for his coffee cup.

"Did you hear me?" I asked.

"I heard you."

"Because no one has slept with you in ten years except for money. And you want to make up some fantasy about me."

"All right," he said, sharply, and glared at me, and meant it, and I backed down.

But I'm sure that part never made it into the story he told Carmine.

These are the games that keep us in some kind of relation to one another. Carmine accuses me of affairs with her friends and family in order to make me feel better about myself. Edgar, her brother, persists in his story that we slept together, out of some twisted sense of connection to his sister, or to me, or to both.

Carmine's mother, Edna, also lives with us, and I ask you, how can a man of uncertain confidence make love to his aging wife when the crone she will soon become is haunting the corridors of their house in her spit-stained house robe and moaning in her sleep at night?

Edna, a good woman, is nevertheless loud, due to deafness, and flatulent, due to constant indigestion. She has a problem keeping her dress buttoned and sometimes forgets to wear underwear. Once she appeared in my bathroom door wearing nothing but a tee shirt, completely disoriented, not at all aware of the shocking way in which she was exposing her bit of muff. Her withered flanks shuddered as she stepped hurriedly out of the door when she saw me, a blur in front of her, no doubt, since she was wearing no glasses. Her pubic hair was prodigious and gray, like underbrush or a thicket. Creeping back along the wall, she vanished.

Last week after Carmine told me she wanted a divorce, I crept into the house again after she was gone. I had no money, nowhere to go. Sitting in front of the computer, I contemplated the web page for Virility Pro, as seen on Time, CNN, ABC, and other places. Medically proven Virility Pro Pills would enlarge my penis naturally, believe it or not! A busty woman of divine smoothness, wearing a thong bikini, knelt in a low tide in the wet sand and looked over her shoulder at me, a glance that said, "Take this pill and you'll be able to do everything I need." I wanted to order the pills, to have them work and write my own customer testimonial. "These pills made me so much larger that I can actually see myself at last! Says Charley S. of Blanktown, State of South Blankana."

Even more professional in appearance was the page for Alpha Male Plus, where I learned that deep in Canada lives an animal scientists believe to be the most prolific lover in the entire animal kingdom, the male Wapiti Elk, *cervus elaphus*. The pill was red. A picture of a handsome man in doctor's clothes looked out at me. The doctor was blonde, with full, red lips. The page included a chart comparing the sexual performance of the average middle-aged male with the average middle-aged Wapiti Elk, and we humans, alas, fell woefully short.

Sex you'll talk about for weeks.

In the case of an erection that lasts over four hours, please seek medical help.

I pictured myself with my true love, the girl in the commercial about the cell phone, whose face I could no longer remember very clearly, so that she occasionally morphed into Halle Berry or, sometimes, Catherine Zeta-Jones. Under the effects of Wapiti Elk hormone, I show her the time of her life. We are in front of the gigantic fireplace in Shangri-la in the movie *Citizen Kane*. Sex is just as good in black-and-white as it is in Technicolor. We're pawing at one another for hours, and Halle/Catherine never even considers using a vibrator.

In the background I can hear Deutze cleaning the house. She'll stop to smoke a cigarette soon, work a while, smoke another, and so on, for another three or four hours. She'll come again in three days. The next check I write her will bounce. If all goes well, she'll be the one to find Carmine's body. She'll be the first to know.

The Last Days of the Golden Age

IN THE LAST WEEK before I realized I was going to lose my job, in the spring of 2002, I was meeting with a new hospital client, trying to sell the administration on upgrading their mainframe-based financial information systems with something that ran on Windows servers and a Windows application called ReadyDoc. By then news of the Enron scandal was eating into the confidence of all my clients, and I could already feel these folks, a Director of Patient Billing and a Director of Patient Financial Services, edging away from me. The name of the place was the Hospital of the Holy Virgin St. Mary in some town called St. Cloud, Minnesota, or someplace like that. I was traveling a lot in the Midwest and was not always sure which state I was in. As the senior consultant in charge of convincing people to give us business, I mostly called on new clients. We at Arthur Andersen were always anxious for more health care business, though times were getting harder and visits tougher as the Enron situation wore on.

As an Arthur Andersen consultant I had a good bit of influence over which computer products my clients bought when they looked to upgrade their billing systems. Every hospital has to upgrade its financial systems in order to have any hope of collecting third-party reimbursement with the kind of efficiency that will keep a hospital or medical practice in business. Every hospital hires consultants to tell their staff how to do this in spite of the fact that the consultants have rarely done any real work in years whereas the hospital's own billing staff does billing every day.

ReadyDoc was a piece of crap that I had sold to a lot of places, after the appropriate bidding process had taken place, and after I had helped my client evaluate the proposals and found that, once again, ReadyDoc was the only answer, along with its partner software package, MediPrik, which took care of tracking laboratory tests, including results and charges, and which offered the best integrated solution for any customer considering the purchase of ReadyDoc. After we had secured this add-on, it would turn out we also needed to integrate RadiShok, to handle X-ray studies and their billings, and then PharmaCop, for the hospital's pharmacy business. Arranging these deals required that we woo and court lots of hospital administrators and doctors, a painful process which included any number of gourmet meals at expensive restaurants. These software products were all coincidentally available from the same vendor, MushySoft Software Medical Division, where we had a lot of friends. MushySoft would sell and install the systems while we supervised the installation, helped set up planning meetings with all departments, and worked on training. With health care costs rising every year in double digits, consultants like us were riding a boom that might never end.

At Holy Virgin we were still trying to get in the door. We were finished with the PowerPoint presentation my Bright Assistant had prepared, and were about to start the getting-to-know-you chat with the Patient Financial Services guy. We were moving out of a conference room and into the Financial Services Office when we heard on a radio at a secretary's desk the news that Arthur Andersen's Chief Executive Officer had resigned.

We got through the meeting. My Bright Assistant's name was Alix Nixon. I was supposed to be showing her the way a client call like this should go but instead we sat in the meeting stunned. We chatted uncomfortably a few minutes and the hospital said good-bye to us. We got very drunk in the airport as the Airport Network played the news over and over again, not just the news about Arthur Andersen but Enron, the whole mess.

Within a few weeks most of the company dissolved as our clients fled to other accountants. My job abandoned me, left me stranded like a starfish in an ebbing tide.

My last day of work fell in late May, 2002. This is what Carmine refers to as being out of work for three years. Clearly this is two years, at the most. It's now 2004, and May is months away, so even if I say two years, I'm giving her a few months. Two years is not three years but you can't tell Carmine. When I point this out, she says I was afraid I was going to be fired for a whole year before that, which is where the third year comes from. So, as usual, she's right, as far as she's concerned.

When you are reduced to a squabble like that one, whether you have been out of work for two years or three and by whose reckoning, your life has come to a pretty sorry pass. But added to that, when you dig in your heels and refuse to back down from your side of the argument, you know that something more aggressive is really happening. The argument is only a disguise.

We begin the argument again when she gets home. This is the night before the day on which I plan to kill her. She's getting ready to go out to the club with her friends. We still have a club membership for the next month or so. I used to play golf there when I could show my face. I haven't told Carmine how broke we are but she's figuring it all out on her own. She's about to go to the club and charge a dinner on my tab, which she knows I can't pay, but she's lecturing me about the work ethic.

"You think I can't count?" I say. "It's March, 2004. I was let go from my job in May 2002. That's less than two years. To get you to two years I'm being generous."

"What a crumb," she says, flinging up her hands, "with your two years instead of three. Like that makes a difference."

"I looked hard for work. I spent weeks taking that fucking real estate course."

"And you lost that job within three months."

"I'm not a real estate person."

"Then why did you spend all that time in the course?"

"To keep you off my back. With your constant, 'It's years you've been out of work, Charley, what's the matter with you? All your friends from Arthur Andersen got good jobs.'"

"They did," she says, hands on her hips. She's wearing bronze-colored push-up pants or whatever they're called, the pants that come down about halfway the calf. The blue veins are showing in the lower part of her legs, driving her crazy. She's blotting the veins with makeup that makes her lightly freckled skin appear oddly blurred.

"The fuck they got good jobs. Mickelson's working nights at the Seven-Eleven on the interstate."

"That's not a Seven-Eleven, it's a Party Pantry."

"Well, whatever. He's selling cigarettes through a little slide window. You want me selling cigarettes out a depressing little slide window at the side of a store?"

"You just don't get it, Charley. You just don't get it. A man works, Charley. A man brings money into the house. It's nice when a woman can help with that but it's a man's job and that's the way it is."

"What are you telling me, you think I don't know this? 'It's a man's job.' Fuck you, with your 'it's a man's job.' When did you ever bring a dime into this house? Even one thin lousy dime?"

"You are out of control, Charley."

"Listen to you. How dare you." I am breathless, speechless with rage, and I sit in the chair where she's piled her dirty clothes. She glares at me but I go on sitting. "How dare you."

"How dare you sit on my dresses like they're common rags."

"I bought these dresses. You lousy bitch."

She clicks her tongue in that way that drives me crazy, that makes me want to take her by the back of the head and slam her face into a wall, that condescending click of the tongue and her hips in those bronze pants, her desperate pants trying to find some way to cling to her ass as she clip-clops out of the room, a movie star diva on an exit line.

I follow her to the dining room.

Framed in the window, backlit against the pool, she says, low, "I want to have a good time with my friends. Don't try to spoil it before I even get out the door."

"Which friends?"

"What business is that of yours?"

"You're probably meeting that golf coach of yours. Or that guy who used to be your personal trainer back when you were going to run the marathon. Remember?"

"Fuck you, Charley," she says. "It was a 10k race and I could have done it if my husband had supported me the way a husband is supposed to." She sails out the door in a full blaze of her own martyrdom. She's unshakeable.

At my old office in Arthur Andersen, one wall was glass and had a great view of the parking deck. The view was of the top of the deck, the edges lined with planters, a lot of English ivy growing out. I expect it was English ivy though it might have been Boston ivy. My own car was parked in another deck and I never actually saw the planters or the ivy up close. The green had a nice, planty kind of look from thirty stories up. Cars crawled around like animated toys. I stood at the window, looking down at the tiny people getting out of the tiny cars and tried to calculate the probable value of the cars that I could see, some ridiculous amount of money, maybe a million dollars right there in front of me.

Since there was no more Bright Assistant, I had to pack my office myself. I'd stopped on the way to work to snag some boxes from behind a liquor store, and one of the boxes smelled of spilt Jack Daniels.

My mind was still full of the useful work of my employment, and I thought with satisfaction of the dozens, nay, scores of times I had convinced hospitals to purchase not only MediPrik but even PathoDirge, our fully automated Windows-compatible pathology reporting-and-charge-capture system. Even if Arthur Andersen was crumpling like an empty circus tent, I still had the fond memories of all the clients whose lives I had thoroughly muddled over the years. I still had all that I had accomplished in the free market. I would live to consult again, there could be no doubt.

I had no intention of telling Carmine until I absolutely had to and to this day she thinks I was actually fired two weeks later.

But today I was walking my liquor boxes full of bits of

personal memorabilia down to my car. All my company files had been seized and carted away. My computer had been absent my desk a week or longer. Even then a security guard would check my boxes as I walked them down to my Lexus.

A few minutes ago I'd met with my boss and signed my severance agreement.

A few minutes from now would fall my deadline for leaving the premises.

In the Lifetime version of my divorce, there is a cut to a dream-scene in which I take up my chair as if it weighs nothing, smash it through the glass window and send it hurtling to the deck far below, into one of the planters of ivy, and I leap to join it. Or, rather, the actor, Mark-Paul Gosselaar, leaps out a window and a stunt double takes the long dive to the top of the parking deck. We follow the fall to the final moment of impact and then the camera snaps back, we realize it was all a dream.

My boss is played by Judith Light and she's the one who bursts in the door and sees the window smashed, the office eerily windswept, and my body flattened on the roof of a mid-size Mercedes many floors below. She walks to the window with incredible grace and looks down. A thousand emotions in the set of her eyes, the waiting. Or is that hyperbole? Do humans even experience a thousand emotions in a lifetime?

Prelude to a recession, the fall of Enron and Arthur Andersen acts as a kind of overture to the collapse of World-Com, to an economic slide that puts hundreds of thousands of people out of work. All this as a result of my having sold inferior software to too many hospitals nationwide. I therefore carry a general sense of being at fault for the whole mess.

Carmine's brother Edgar lost his job during this same

recession, but in his case, he'd only held it for fourteen months. He thought a year ago he'd found his vocation as a Kinko's shift supervisor. Now he's looking for a lawyer to help him file a discrimination lawsuit. He says they fired him because he came to work in a kilt.

The office still felt like mine as I closed the door. I had a flash of an image from that last meeting with Holy Virgin. The Director of Patient Billing was a pale, rouged, gaudily-scarved woman in a turquoise suit and turquoise print blouse with large turquoise buttons. She appeared to flinch every time I said the word, "MediPrik." The memory might have made me laugh if this had not been the last time I was closing the door of my office. Marooned out of the life I thought I had been making for myself, I looked at the carpet, stained from my coffee, my muddy shoes, my flecks of skin and bits of hair. Who could be more melancholy, more forlorn? Who could move more unnoticed, more neglected, among all the other unemployed? Who could think more of himself at such a moment? Who, indeed, but me?

Purchase

IN THE TWO WEEKS following my departure from Arthur Andersen, while Carmine remained ignorant that I was now a no-good out-of-work bum like all the rest, I spent money like it was about to go extinct. We bought a new Capresso coffee robot even more expensive than the old one, which we gave to Annette. I got new golf clubs, a new riding lawn mower, and a new stereo for my home office. We moved our boat to a more expensive slip at the marina, one I'd been trying to get for years. I knew perfectly well I would be selling the boat pretty soon, but even then I took the more expensive space, just to have the prestige of it for a few more weeks.

I bought a nice Gucci suit that looks like a sack on me but that looked great when I saw it on Ben Affleck.

Carmine is never one to be outdone in the shopping arena, and when she saw what kind of mood I was in she decided to redo the kitchen and buy new furniture for the guest house, which is in back of the pool house. So we bought a bed made out of Swedish memory foam once used in a NASA program, and she shopped relentlessly for other excessively stark pieces to match the idea of the bed.

I slept in the guest house the night I told her I had lost my job. The Swedish foam space-bed had not yet arrived, but I had the old bed with its tired innerspring mattress. Carmine was sobbing hysterically on the phone with her sister, Eileen, who lives in Brussels with her diplomatic corps husband.

A phone sat on the night table by the bed in the guest house, but I realized with a lurch that there was nobody I could call except my children. My wife had kicked me out of my own house for the night and I had no one to talk to about it. Parents dead, God bless them both. No brothers or sisters. All my friends from work gone the way of all friends from work, especially when work was the subject of a public scandal. So I could call my son Frank and disturb him from his duties as a young banker and family man, or I could call Annette and disturb her in the precious quiet of late night, with her skinny girlfriend passed out from hunger in the next room.

I sat on the bed, which creaked with a metallic welcome. Was this really true, was there really nobody I could call?

Throughout this crisis I had begun drinking steadily more; I had always enjoyed alcohol too much, though I usually did my heavy drinking away from the house. Tonight, I thought, I would drink at home.

Sneaking into the kitchen, I poured myself a stiff vodka. I fiddled with the new coffee machine for a while but still could not figure out how to turn it on. I drank the vodka.

At the top of the stairs sounded a ringing voice. "Charley, that better not be you, bum that you are, in my kitchen. Get out of my house. Get out."

I waited for her heavy footfall on the carpeted step, a sound I knew well, and slipped out the back door with my drink, my ice, my bottle.

A person's mind forages for comfort on well-beaten paths. Even then, I was thinking that if I could only buy the perfect gift for Carmine, I could make everything right. Even with Carmine as angry as she was, with a good gift I stood a fifty-fifty chance.

Maybe she would want a piece of jewelry. Or maybe that would seem like a reminder of our love, the taste of which went a bit sour in the mouth at the moment. At any rate, jewelry was entirely too portable.

She hated every dress I ever bought her, even the ones she picked out, until she had exchanged them at least twice. So giving her a dress risked that we would both forget what the gift was for by the time she found something she liked.

In fact, it is my firm belief that Carmine hated every dress she ever bought the week after she had worn it the first time. She also had a rule about shoes, which was that I was never to buy her any.

Maybe we could both go away on a trip together, somewhere more practical than the pilgrimage to the Holy Land she was always talking about. Neither of us had ever seen the Grand Canyon, for instance. We could explore it together, a trip west, symbolic of the need for change. People's lives are often transformed by trips west, especially to scenic vistas like those available near the Grand Canyon. Such a fitting end to this troubled period of our lives would become possible there, the two of us reconciled in spite of our troubles, facing an uncertain future but steadfast in our devotion to one another.

From where I was sitting I could suddenly hear her voice, and to make sure I caught every word, she'd opened the windows with her own two hands, when for twenty years it's been, "Charley, would you get the window? You know my back."

Now she was screaming into the phone at the top of her lungs. "Because he is a no-good bum, Eileen. All that bullshit about being kept on to help close down the company. A pile of I don't know what. A word I can't say in front of our mother, who is also standing right here, looking at me like we're both about to be homeless in the street."

She had an artful way of setting the scene, not only for her sister Eileen but for me and for any of the nearer neighbors who might be listening. A voice like the rasp edge of a saw.

"What do I know whether he did anything wrong? He's been afraid of getting fired for a year, can you believe it? A whole year of this, and now it's really happened. Thank God we have a little savings.

"Well, I don't know what I thought. I thought he was just exaggerating. How would I know? Sure, he'll find another job. What, me? What could I do? For God's sake. Look at you, talking to me about getting a job when you never worked a day in your life. I didn't say I was any different. I said I didn't say I was any different. You're upsetting Mother. She's upset, she's walking out of the room, she's shaking her head. She's shaking her head at you, not at me.

"What if we have to go to the shelter, Eileen? What do you mean, calm? How can I be calm? Sure, there's money, for now. For now. Eileen? Eileen? Whose sister are you? Let me ask you, whose sister are you in the first place?" She reached, one-handed, and snapped the window closed.

I could buy her another fur coat. She adored fur in spite of her morbid fear of animal rights activists who might hurl ink at her in public; for this reason she rarely wore the chinchilla she already owned.

Or I could buy her that rock and water feature she'd been wanting for the living room, an installation by some Japanese artist who arranged rocks, water, and sand in pricey combinations, with one of those circulating pumps that kept the water gushing like a waterfall. She'd had the photo, from her friend Amir's house, on her dresser for the last six months, face up, where I could see it whenever I passed.

After consideration, the rock and water feature was taking on the air of a favorite, though it was sure to cost a lot of money. We should be watching our pennies now that I was out of work, now that we were living on my unemployment and my savings.

Our savings. Though I earned all the money. For some reason I feel I must keep pointing out this fact, even though, back when we decided Carmine would be a stay-at-home wife, I vowed our marriage was still a partnership and swore I wanted her to stay at home, had never pictured her working. Those words actually came out of my mouth.

"I can be for women's lib and still stay at home," Carmine reflected. "Don't you think?"

"I don't see any contradiction."

This was from a conversation a very long time ago, maybe the second year of our marriage. She had been working as an elementary school teacher up until then, but my salary was already enough to support us both. We were still living in that apartment on Baker Heights Avenue, sitting on that flowered sofa. I was in a state of shock. I had just told Carmine, who probably still called herself Lauren at the time, to quit her job, and even though I had clearly said the words of my own volition I wasn't quite sure why. Carmine was sitting beside me with her tiny hands folded so sweetly in her lap. At the time she was young and smooth and shiny and very petite, the height of her beauty, while my twenty-five minutes as a good-looking young man were already over. I was very aware of the difference between us in terms of attractiveness. This difference has shrunk since then, but at the time it was pretty marked. Lauren sat blinking next to me, demure as a sleeping kitten. "You're so good to me, Charley."

"You can sit here all day and read books about women's lib, if that makes you feel better."

"I'm sure I'll be all right after I get used to it," she said. "I'm so lucky. My sister Eileen is supporting her husband through law school, she's working all the time, poor thing." Which was true, of course, and which brought into question the aforementioned accusation that sister Eileen "never worked a day in [her] life." Not that I want to bring up every little fact that Carmine gets wrong.

Years later, jobless, sitting in the guest house listening to the edges of Carmine's harangue, I heard my cell phone ring on the night stand beside me. The sound startled me, as if I had never heard the ringtone before. Salvation, in spite of my doubt! Here was a friend from work, perhaps, or even Frank or Ann, who had heard about their father's misfortune and called to show their support. I picked up the receiver hopefully, said hello, and a few minutes later pledged fifty bucks to the local Fraternal Order of the Police.

In the silence after the call, I failed to make any headway in any direction that led toward standing up or leaving that room. My life was ringing with disaster fallen on it like a fresh ax. I couldn't make any headway against the premonition of more disaster to come. I sat like a lump of lead that was once a lump of gold.

But a man doesn't maintain a paunch the size of mine by sitting around drinking cocktails in a room with a creaky bed. I headed to the kitchen to steal something to eat.

While I was creeping along the holly bushes, unfriendly sharp buggers that they are, I was thinking about what it would be like to call my brother, for instance. If I had a brother, what a nice thing that would be. Even if my brother hated me, he would still have to listen to me. Even if he thought I was the biggest loser, whiner, and deadbeat on the planet, which I felt like at the moment, he would still have to talk to me. If he didn't, I'd call my mother and tell on him. If my mother were alive.

Bathed in my own pathos, I slathered mayonnaise onto whole wheat bread in the dark. Either the refrigerator light had burned out or Carmine had unscrewed it, and I could see only vague blurs of packages and jars on the shelves. I dared not turn on any lights in the room and was trying to make as little noise as possible, but at the same time noticed that I was drifting a bit to the lee each time I took a forward step, as if I were moving against a considerable current.

I thought what I made was a turkey, lettuce, and tomato sandwich, with a slice of Swiss cheese, but when I arrived at my poolside bungalow I discovered something much more ominous, combining liver cheese, pepperjack cheese, and cabbage. There was at least tomato, fresh and ripe. I threw away the cabbage and learned to love the rest.

From upstairs drifted no longer the echo of the bellow of the harridan. Now there wafted down to me a rhythmic sound rather like sobbing. Carmine was the very fount of tears and could weep like a lost soul for hours, all the while working a book of crossword puzzles. I listened to her with a certain amount of tugging going on in and about my cardiac region. No doubt she was as frightened as I was under the layers of our two performances, for I was struck, being drunk and open to profundity, by the way we had both become caricatures of ourselves.

If I were a religious man I would have had a religious specialist to call. I could have chatted with my rabbi, my priest, my imam. Any visiting shaman would have worked fine for me, as long as he or she could by intuition figure out to dial my number in my hour of need. This was the kind of self-centered person I had become; you would have to find me to help me, I wouldn't lift a finger until you did.

The perfect gift for Carmine was nearly always a new car of one kind or another. We had been married twenty-six years and I must have bought her fifteen cars. She had the two-door, the minivan, the first SUV off the line, she had the Mercedes S-class, the Subaru Outback. At that moment she had two cars, the S-class Mercedes and a Hybrid something or other from Toyota. She mostly drove the S-class except when she attended certain greener kind of functions in which case she drove the hybrid. She pretended to want to give the Mercedes to Ann but only because she knew I would never, ever agree to it and therefore she could keep both cars.

At the time a first wave of new-SUV longing was sweeping over her, I'd already begun to notice it before my crisis. Maybe I could buy her a new car. The picture was beginning to clear.

As I had been doing for the last two weeks, I reviewed all the money I had in any bank, anywhere. All the stocks, the bonds, the money markets which hardly earned anything. I'd saved a lot. Enough to keep us for two good years without even slowing down, and surely by then I would have a job. I'd better. Carmine was hardly built for hard times, and neither was I.

If we sold the S-class and the Hybrid. No, just the S-class. And bought her a new Lexus SUV. I'd seen the way she thirsted for one when we were watching the commercials, the fleet, lone, streamlined body tearing along the solitary Western highway, not a building or automobile in sight, and

Carmine picturing herself at the wheel, shifting effortlessly, though in real life she drives an automatic.

It always comes down to some kind of purchase, to some exchange involving the market. We hurt one another in some way, or some disaster happens, and in response we buy something. We need to say how happy we are due to some great occasion, like a wedding or the birth of a child, and to express ourselves we buy something. We lose a loved one or a friend loses a loved one and in response we purchase some service or buy some card or offer some gift of food, traded for money, one way or another, because it is the medium of all exchange. The solution to any problem always returns us to the market.

I would have to go to the market to appease Carmine. I would have to go to the market more than once. At some local dealership I would haggle uncertainly with the Lexus salesman of the moment until we reached an agreeable bargain involving two cars and a considerable amount of cash. This offering of peace I would give to Carmine to assure her that nothing would change in our lives due to my unemployment. Like all our transactions in the past, this one would be based on shaky moral principles, including my presumption that Carmine would flee if I could not give her the material life she wanted. Also including my presumption that Carmine would act out of the worst part of her character now that she knew I had no job. In our marriage, there had never been any question of pulling together to do anything; the money had done everything for us, there had never been any reason to make much of an effort.

I would also have to go to the market with myself, too, and no longer fresh or new, bright as this year's penny; I would be that dull penny from years ago, shunted from pocket to pocket. To find another job I would have to make a transaction of myself, announce to the market that I was available, openly flaunting my charms via whatever media I could bend to the task. The finest résumé papers and envelopes. The most thoroughgoing job listing websites. Conspicuously perfect attendance at all my outplacement counseling sessions. Immaculate grooming at all times. I was my only product, and I was once again available for purchase.

O Market which art in heaven, hallowed be thy name. Where we shall shop in eternal happiness and find countless tasteful products. Where we shall never need to talk to each other but only to give each other presents. O Market of Markets, hear oh Israel, the Lord your God is one Market. As it was sold in the beginning, it is so sold now and ever shall be, Market without end. Amen.

Even then, I was beginning to feel the divine nature of Markets, which expand and contract without regard to human emotion, which answer only to the higher laws of competition and natural selection. Perhaps all the Eastern religions are wrong, along with all the Western ones. God is not everywhere all at once, he is not some vibration sounding through the universe. God is not an all-seeing all-knowing anything. God is a Market. God is The Market, the free one, of course.

If I were religious and had the aid of a religious professional, I would be able to pray. Right there in the guest house with the light moving strangely on the ceiling, reflected from the surface of the pool. I could get on my knees and ask the religious professional to say something appropriate to open this dialogue. I would pour out my heart in comfortable increments to a God who would reward me with solace, peace of mind, and a guarantee of a new job at the same salary as before.

Arthur Andersen had failed the Market and paid a great price. How much of that price was laid on my head, personally? Was my debt paid by my present unemployment or was there still more to come?

In purchasing a gift for Carmine, I would not only be appeasing her sense of our place in the world, I would also be appeasing The Market. Making a transaction as an offering would allow me to apologize for any way in which I had failed The Market, too, along with Arthur Andersen and Enron. Ways in which I had failed personally and debts which I personally would have to pay.

At the time there was sparse furniture in the guest house. We had moved a lot of the old junk out to make room for the new furniture that would be arriving along with the Swedish foam bed. I was sitting in the dark pretty much too drunk to find a light switch. I'd finished eating the sandwich and was waiting for something else to do.

Somehow I managed to turn on the TV, or maybe it had been on all along. It was not at all unusual to walk into a room in our house and find a TV playing and no one watching; maybe this TV had been playing all night and I'd never once registered what was on the screen. Maybe it had been playing for months and no one had ever noticed.

The alcohol altered my hearing a bit, adding a quality of drippiness and ringiness, as if all sound in the world were being filtered through someone's bathroom pipes.

A cool hand lay on my forehead, rested there quite gently, asking for nothing. Perfect cool smooth skin touched mine, and called something out of me. I opened my eyes, expecting it was Carmine, expecting she had calmed down and was ready to talk.

The person who was sitting there, though, was Sigourney Weaver in the outfit from *Aliens*, the second movie in the Alien series, where she saves the blond hunk Marine played by Michael Biehn and the little blonde girl played by Little

Blonde Girl only to have them both die in the wait for the third episode. The person sitting here was Sigourney Weaver but as that version of Ripley still with a bit of hope remaining, not yet the completely despairing Ripley of *Aliens III* or the monster Ripley of IV. She was holding an automatic rifle and pointed it at my head. The tip was so cold it sucked all the heat out of my body just by touching me. "You want me to do it?"

"Do what?"

"Pull the trigger. Wise up. This is a movie, we don't have all day."

"This is not a movie. I just lost my job, here."

"So I guess you want a look at my tits," Sigourney said.

"Please just shoot me," I said. "Go ahead and shoot me."

"Oh, come on. My tits can't be that bad."

"You know what I mean. I deserve to die. Pull the trigger."

"I should," she said. "Before that thing comes crawling out of you." She smiles a smile so sinister it might indeed have come out of Ripley in IV. "You looking for some kind of sympathy?"

"My wife won't even talk to me."

"She must have liked your job."

"I liked my job," I said.

As usual, Weaver wasn't showing much emotion on the surface, a kind of elfin bemusement in the expression, with something dangerous in the set of the jaw and the placement of the teeth, just visible between parted lips. "You'll get another one. That's how it works, right? I finish one movie, I get another one."

"One of these days they'll kill Ripley and she won't come back."

"You think so?" She's amused at the thought, not in the least threatened.

"Or some other actor will play her. Someone younger."

That hit home. I could see it. But the placid expression settled over her face again. "I'm a visitation," she said. "Don't piss me off."

"Sorry."

"I'm your warning that things could get really strange from here on out."

She shoved the gun into my mouth and pulled the trigger. Nothing happened except that the next moment she wasn't there any more, and I was looking around trying to remember where I was and it came to me that this was the guest house next to the pool house but it was also more or less the dog house and I was in it and I had apparently passed out and hallucinated for a while.

I blinked myself awake, trying to remember the vision I had been having, the actual presence of a movie star with a semi-automatic weapon shoved into my mouth.

Was I going to buy Carmine a car? Was that what I had decided?

From the house, the dead silence of early morning was almost throbbing around me, and when I stumbled onto the lawn my socks were soaked with dew. I stood there blinking with sodden feet looking at the back of the house, no lights, all blank and dark. Carmine had taken an Ambien and gone to bed. Why couldn't I take an Ambien, too?

Forty Whacks

SIPPING VODKA AND LIME, I'm sitting in the hot tub, soaking in the strawberry stuff that Carmine keeps around for her baths. Pretty soon we won't be able to afford the strawberry stuff or, probably, the mortgage payment on the house that holds the hot tub, and the thought of losing everything I've worked for all my life is rolling around my head, making it harder to relax in the hot water than it should be.

Into the bathroom walks my daughter Ann. I'm covered with foam to my chin but the vaguely shadowy naked parts of my body under the water are still visible and I cover myself automatically with my hand. "Look at you," she says, "all bubbly. When did you start using Mom's bubble bath?"

"I'm having some quiet time," I say. "You have no business coming into the bathroom when I'm in here."

She waves her hand at me dismissively, the expensive gleam of her nails catching my eye, as it is meant to do. Her five-thousand-dollar breasts are shoved out nicely against her pink tube top. Ann has my Aunt Maureen's shape: no waist, wide hips, and thick, square shoulders. For high school she asked for breast surgery so we bought her a pair of breasts that sit on her chest like wanton grapefruit, unnaturally firm on a body that has never done an hour's worth of labor in its twenty-odd years of life. "Please, Pa. I'm old enough to see you in the bathroom. Besides, there's soap scum on the water and you've got your hand over yourself so what are you complaining about?"

She proceeds to take out a cigarette and light it, sucking the smoke back into her mouth, attempting to look bored. She has spent the majority of her life trying to perfect this look.

"A man could use a little privacy in his own bathroom."

"You have nothing but privacy, Pa, you don't have a job."

"I need you to remind me of this."

She waved her hand at me again. "I need some money for the weekend."

"What?"

"Give me some money."

"I don't have any money with me right now, Annette, I'm in the bathtub. Do you see?"

"It's a Jacuzzi."

"Whatever."

She is wearing a style of shoe made famous on *Sex and the City*, and her hair is rippled and highlighted and styled like Sarah Jessica Parker's; she appears to be posing, now, perched on the toilet with the seat top lowered and her jeans-clad legs splayed on the rug. She has a crease in the jeans, which are always dry-cleaned and pressed, and the bottoms are rolled partway up her calves. "So Papa, why come you never abused your daughter. You think I'm ugly?"

"Why did I what? What kind of question is that?" I take a good pull from the vodka.

"So many dads abuse their daughters. Look at *Law & Order*. There was an episode last night with a dad who constantly had sex with his daughter." She's chewing some kind of gum, studying her nails, occasionally sitting upright to study herself in the mirror. She glares at me with the defiant pout of a teenybopper. She's in one of her I-want-to-shock-you moods. "Why come you never tried with me?"

"You're asking me this while I'm naked in the bathtub with my hand over my privates."

"You think I'm ugly, don't you?"

She is sitting there with boobs I paid for and a nose I paid for and liposuction that I paid for and she wants to know what I think of the bargain I got.

"You're a beautiful girl," I say, smacking my lips. I wish for a touch of grapefruit juice in my cocktail. I'm so mellow the room is starting to swim, the little fishes on the wallpaper wriggling and wavering.

"Were you ever tempted? I mean, it would have been creepy if you ever tried anything but it would be okay if you had dirty thoughts about me. And, you know, like, you fought them off."

"Please, Ann, young lady. No. I never entertained any thoughts of that kind about you. Of the abusive father kind, I mean."

She has begun to pout. This might be a genuine emotional response or an attempt to change her reflection in the mirror. When she sits up straight to check herself out again, and primps her hair a bit, I figure it's another pose. "Maybe you're gay," she says.

"You've been talking to your mother."

"Did you ever have any thoughts about Frank?"

Frank is her brother, a no-good banker who lives never mind where but pretty close and never bothers to come to visit his parents. Since I lost my job you'd think I was poison to my own son. God forbid I should spoil his perfect life with what's her name Ramona with the hair processed nineteen different ways. "You have a sick imagination," I say.

"Why would Mom make up that you're gay, Pa?"

"I should know why your mother would do anything?"

She rolls her eyes and cocks her head. She's being careful to keep her eyes away from the bathtub and the fading suds. "Point," she says. "So, you going to give me some money?"

"What do you need money for?"

"I have to get my nails done this afternoon and I can't pay."

"Why can't you pay? You have a job."

"I don't have a shift tonight and I spent my cash." She's an actress who never works, which means she waits tables and lives on her tips and on handouts from me. She pouts again, attempting to look even younger and more childish. On the face of a twenty-eight-year-old this is unattractive. The pout squashes her features toward the center and makes her face look more like a moon pie. I miss her old nose, which was long enough to give the face some character. She had the boobs done for high school and the nose after college, so I remember the old nose better than the old boobs. "Papa. Please. I just need fifty dollars."

"A nail job costs fifty dollars?"

"I need to buy some makeup, too."

My hands are twitching in the water like my wallet is at the bottom of the tub and I'm going to reach down to find it full of waterlogged hundred dollar bills. Ann's little girl routine is as tired as my scalp. For a last moment I am the father who always managed to find a few dollars for his daughter; then it's a moment later and I realize there's nothing in my wallet, or in the bank, or anywhere.

"Get out of the bathroom so I can finish my bath, Ann." Even to me my voice sounds different. There's a timbre, a depth, that comes out of my deepest gut; just a note, a sounding, but I hear it. Someplace deep down in myself, I hear the change. I feel tired, close my eyes.

She swings her legs and kicks at the stainless steel trash basket. She is feeling my discomfort and, in a shocking display of sensitivity, is teetering on the verge of becoming concerned for me.

From rooms away comes the drone of a television set, the peculiar rhythm and sound effects of the evening news. My heart is pounding. "Who's that?" I ask.

"Hilda, my friend."

"The skinny one."

"She's anorexic, Papa. You're not supposed to mention she's skinny." An expression of relief crowds out the concern that Ann was starting to feel; easier to scold me than to worry about me. "Honestly. It's not like she can help being thin."

"Sure she could. She could eat a cookie."

"Keep your voice down. I'm trying to help her with that."

"What's so hard? You eat a sandwich and you don't stick your finger down your throat."

"Shut up. Gross. I didn't say she was bulimic." She is relaxed again, more like her old self. At the corner of her eyes the merest beginnings of a crease. She has her mother's skin, fine and prone to wrinkles. She picks up one of her mother's scented soaps and slips it into her blouse pocket.

She looks at me hard when she gets up. An uncharacteristic wrinkle of concern down the center of her brow. I am trying to shrink into the water and cover myself with my hands again. "I'm sorry I barged in on you."

"No problem. As long as I don't get out of the water I won't scar you for life, right?"

She laughs, but only in a half-hearted way. "You all right, Pa?"

"Me?" I do a partly underwater shrug. "I'm fine."

"You sure?"

"I'll make it."

She twists from side to side, the way she did when she was twelve and wanted twenty dollars for makeup. "Mom's serious about the divorce," she says. "She means it this time."

"I know she does, sweetie. You don't have to worry about that."

"Do you need any money?" Ann asks, then blushes. "I mean, how are things for you?"

I stare at my toes at the far end of the water. "We'll get by. I got a couple of interviews next week."

She brightens, backing toward the door; a towel with a melon motif is hanging there, and she opens the door by pulling on the towel. "That's good. You haven't had any interviews for a while." But she doesn't ask what jobs I'm interviewing for, what companies, any of the questions that immediately spring to mind. She's staring obstinately at the tile of the bathroom floor.

"Maybe my luck's turning," I say.

"Sure, Papa. I hope so."

"Now, why don't you go outside and wait for me to get out of the tub, sweetheart."

"I need to run," she says. "I'll let myself out. See you."

"Take the skinny girl with you, get her something to eat."

When she's gone the room is curiously empty, the slight

splashes of the water amplified by the fact that my ears are just above the surface. Why did I lie to her?

She was embarrassed to have asked for money, but because I had none to give, not because at her age she should be too proud to beg for my spare change. I've been out of a job for two years and this is the first time it occurs to my daughter that I might be having money problems. This is the person my daughter has become, this child-woman with her dry-cleaned designer blue jeans and her constant need for fifty bucks to pay for a manicure. Fool that I am, I would have given it to her if I had that much cash in my pocket.

I stand up in the tub, steadying myself on one of the fixtures. Water drains off me like music, dripping. In the mirror opposite I can see myself, pale and flabby, nipples sagging on a chest that looks more like breasts than ever. The angle of sag of my man-boobs is about equal to the angle of my belly as it droops downward. My genitals look tiny and forlorn, clenched tightly against my pubic hairs as if they would like to re-ascend into my abdomen. My legs and arms are thin. I look like a potato man, with stick arms and stick legs. I'm the color of chalk with hints of blue where veins shine through the skin. My grizzled body hair lies plastered against the skin. Only my face reminds me of me, but, since I've stopped shaving every day and have a kind of waddle under my chin, I'm not getting much encouragement from studying my expression. I look old and tired and habitually sad.

I flex my arms, watching the stringy biceps attempt to gather and swell. I've been thinking about killing Carmine with an ax. Do I even have the strength to swing one?

I dress and drive to Home Depot to shop for a hatchet. For this purchase I stop for money at an ATM on the way. To my shock the machine won't give me five hundred dollars;

according to the running balance on the bottom of the trans-action record, I only have about a hundred dollars left in the account. I'm stunned, and suddenly afraid. But I withdraw this last bit of cash and look at it, till the person behind me, waiting for the ATM, clears her throat conspicuously. I walk away, sliding the bills into my pocket. There's no more money after this. Since I've always handled the finances, I'm the only one who knows, though Carmine will find out the next time she tries to get money out of the ATM herself. She'll think it's just another screw-up, that all I'll need to do is move more money out of our savings; it will be news to her that our savings are gone, our retirement is gone, our mortgage is in arrears. We're a quarter of an inch from the wall and barreling toward it at top speed. I pocket my cash and head for the hardware store.

It's arguable that in the case of buying an ax with which to murder my wife, I ought to consider shopping at a local, independent hardware dealer; it would be prudent to search out a store of the Mom-and-Pop variety, maybe even to drive to a small, rural town somewhere outside this not-to-be-named suburb in which I live. In a bucolic village hardware store I might purchase a hatchet and leave no computerized record of the transaction whatsoever.

But even as I consider this I see Lennie Briscoe from *Law & Order* showing my black and white Arthur Andersen corporate photo to Mom or Pop, standing behind the manual cash register. "You ever see this guy in here, maybe to buy a maul-type tool like an ax?"

"This guy? Oh yeah, I remember this guy. Drove one of them luxury SUVs from Japan. Seemed real nervous like."

"He give you a name?"

"No, sir, detective. Paid cash. Really sweaty cash, too; I had to leave it out on the counter to dry for a while."

"Can you describe him?"

"You just showed me a picture of him."

"Describe him anyway."

"Ugly fellow. Bald, not quite a comb-over but close. Fat. Never worked a day in his life. Pale, like he came from the city, no offense, sir. Not even one of them fake tans, which, we have a tanning parlor like that right here in Sioux City."

"That must be great for the singles scene," quips Lennie. Behind him is the vaguer outline of his partner, an actor of color, handsome, earnest, athletic in his moderately priced suit. Partner smiles at Lennie's quip.

Cut to me, in the Japanese luxury SUV again, driving to the anonymity of a busy Home Depot on a weekend afternoon.

Home Depot always has a cheerful, high-ceilinged, anything-is-possible feel to it. As I enter the automatic doors, I find myself walking a bit straighter, sucking in my stomach, attempting to appear as though I might actually use some of these burly tools on the shelves. I wander around the windows section, looking at all the different kinds of windows a person can buy. People are buying hot dogs at the stand near the end of the check-out lanes; I am hungry for a hot dog but decide it's better to speak to as few people as possible.

The axes and hatchets are harder to find than I expect and I wander into the garden section, scratching my head beside trays of spring flowers. A young woman wearing a Home Depot apron smiles at me. She has an oval face made arresting by eyes of the coldest blue I have ever seen; she's about as tall as my daughter but has a better proportion, though still a rather generous figure. Her name tag reads "Lizzie." She looks a lot like Elizabeth Montgomery, from *Bewitched*. For a moment she has a perfectly blank, almost frightening expression; then she smiles and a human light floods her features. "Are you looking for help with plants?"

"No, I'm here to shop for a hatchet."

"Here? This is the garden section."

"I wandered in here because of the crowd. I'm not as fond of crowds as I used to be."

"It's only like this on weekends." Lizzie gives me a wide-eyed look that means she is probably wearing contact lenses, though I can't see them. She appears to be watching me but I appear to be standing somewhere else, in her vision. "But I guess that makes sense. Working people can't come here during the week."

"I certainly can't. I have to be at work pretty early in the morning."

She is very curvaceous, coming up to about my shoulder, with a plump shape that has the appearance of solid, firm flesh, not the powdery, cellulitish corpulence of Carmine. Her perfume has an old-fashioned mellow tone, a hint of roses and jasmine. "What kind of work do you do?" she asks.

"Hospital consulting. I'm a billings consultant."

"That sounds interesting."

"I take it you're a garden expert."

"Part-time," she says. However, pride in her finances induces her to explain further. "I only work here for something to do, really. I own some real estate and that's how I make most of my money."

"Real estate."

"I don't trust stocks," she says. "I put my money in houses and land." She has a wicked gleam in her eye when she is discussing her property.

"I wish I had done more of that," I say.

"Were you messed up in the crash?"

I'm not sure which crash she means, but the conversation is beginning to strike a bit close to home. Time for another lie. "I lost a little, not very much. I bought a couple of houses right before stocks went in the tank. I guess I just had a feeling." I scratch my head, giving her something of an earnest look, but a fake one, to match the look of fake friendliness she is giving me.

"Smart," she says. "What does a man like you need with a hatchet?"

I only hesitate a moment. "I'm planning to kill somebody with it."

She nods, hardly blinking. "You'll want something with a wooden handle. Wood gives you a good grip, and you can break off the handle and put in it the fireplace afterwards."

"I don't have a fireplace."

"In the old days you could wash off the hatchet and then cover it with ash to get rid of the blood evidence. These days there's luminol. So I don't know."

"My," I say, "you do seem to know what you're talking about."

"A hatchet would not be my choice any more."

"What would you use?"

"I'd have to think about it," she says, in a noncommittal way. "Poison, maybe."

"Did you ever want to kill somebody?"

She favors me with the most demure little smile. "I don't believe that's a proper question for a gentleman to ask a lady."

My nearness to her is giving me a bit of an erection. She looks so much like Elizabeth Montgomery that I almost ask her what happened to the first Darren; and I am aware of the fact that Montgomery did once play Lizzie Borden in a TV movie. But that doesn't explain the sudden stiffening of my interest. Truth is, a bit of an erection is all I usually have these days, but right now it's feeling fairly functional. Something about her voice, the way it makes the skin at the back of my neck shiver. I am pointing this out here as further proof that I am not gay. "My apologies," I say.

She turns back to her watering, letting fine spray drift over pots of impatiens. I go on standing there waiting for my woody to fade. I suppose she thinks I'm creepy. Just as I'm about to leave, however, she turns back to me for a moment. "You should get a good haircut and maybe lose ten pounds. Appearances are very important if you want to kill somebody and get acquitted."

I look down at the expanse of my belly under the knit shirt I'm wearing. She's being generous; ten pounds wouldn't even make a dent. "I don't have time for a diet but maybe I could get a haircut and a facial," I say.

"In a hurry?"

"Yes."

"Don't be. Be patient, wait for the perfect time. Some quiet morning when you catch her in the right room, and there's nobody around. You'll know when the moment is right."

She turns away again. Those firm round buttocks are fighting against the fabric of her skirt. What a fine thing, to see the ripe shape of a woman's body standing up to her clothing.

She's right, of course. But I don't have enough money left to buy myself the luxury of more time. When I think about the fact that I've got maybe a hundred dollars to my name, a tightness comes to my breathing and I feel as if I need to get outside, in the open, as quickly as I can. This would be a bad place for me to buy an ax, anyway; too many people have seen me talking to Lizzie Borden here. Someone is sure to remember.

I'll use a butcher knife, I think. We already have a couple of those. We have a completely equipped kitchen, just in case anybody who visits us ever wants to cook in it.

Charley Stranger took a knife
and with it finished off his wife
when he saw what he had done
he killed his daughter and his son

"Knife" works just as well as "ax" when it comes to the rhyme scheme for a cute, memorable little ditty. But it's not quite as edgy. I miss the "forty whacks."

In Black and White

THE SITUATION COMEDY VERSION of my family life includes several series of episodes that are revealing about our character as a nuclear unit.

The early episodes are fairly ordinary, nothing America hasn't seen before. In one of the stories, my daughter Ann frets about her looks, her ability to gain a boyfriend, and her possible future married life chattering with her best friend zany Rosie Garner from next door. Ann colors her hair and the end product is a disaster. Her mother and she try to hide it from me in a hideous, laughable wig. They're in a panic before dinner because they're sure I'll never fall for the ruse. But I'm oblivious, lost in my ambition to land a big account at work, and I don't even notice when the wig falls off Ann's head and lands in my lap.

Charley: Your hair sure looks bright, honey.

Ann: Oh Dad, you're so lame.

Carmine: Charley, you moron. I thought you would be furious.

Charley: It'll grow out.

Ann: It looks like a cherry Jolly Rancher.

Carmine: Look at it. Red as my lipstick. And you just sit there and that's all you have to say, Gee Ann, your hair sure looks bright. You'd let her get away with anything. You spoil her.

Charley: What, you want me to slap the kid around because she dyed her hair?

Ann: Mom said it would be all right.

Carmine: Of course I don't want you to slap her around.

Charley: You want me to slap you around?

Following this comes an hilarious, uproarious slapstick teleplay in which Ann wonders whether I pay any attention to her. As part of the story she is baking a disastrous series of pies with her weird friend Vera Tucker from next door, the other next door. They invite zany Rosie over and Mom comes home and finds them busily, industriously at work. Ann asks Mom whether she thinks I even notice her or love her at all. Oh honey, Mom says, your dad's just busy at work, that's all. He's got to make money to take care of us. The episode ends with a terrific pie fight in the kitchen with Rosie and Mom on one side and Ann and Vera on the other. Mom is a dead shot with a tin pie plate and Vera keeps hitting herself in the face. The laugh track cracks me up.

Among my very favorites is one of the "Mom is redecorating the house" episodes, from just after the pie fight, in fact. Mom has bought a very expensive Ch'ing Dynasty vase and has to sneak it into a prominent position in the house without my noticing it, because I'm sure to declare it a lump of useless glass that sits on the carpet, for which a dime store knockoff would have served just as well. In a turn from my usual oblivious state, I notice the vase right away and blow my stack at the price tag in an hilariously predictable way. We'll add a rider on our house insurance, says Mom, in case somebody breaks it, and I grip the top of my head like I'm going to explode. Zany Rosie and Ann are doing their homework in the dining room and have a hard time keeping from laughing. Mom reconciles me to the purchase by fixing me a big gin martini with special cocktail onions from Spain and the whole evening passes splendidly.

Charley: Man. What a good martini.

Carmine: I made it just like you like, stirred, not shaken.

Charley: You put a lot of gin in it, that's the main thing.

Carmine: I wish you would switch to vodka. Everybody in the neighborhood drinks vodka martinis.

Charley: I'm not everybody. I'm my own man. Marching to the tune of a different drummer.

Carmine: Because you drink gin.

Charley: Because I drink gin in a vodka-crazy age.

Carmine: Gin makes a person mean.

Charley: Not Charley.

Carmine: My grandfather was a gin drinker. He was a complete son-of-a-bitch.

"Mom buys a sexy outfit" follows after the one about the vase. Mom is still trying to get back into my good graces. She buys a slinky nightie from Victoria's Secret and shows it to weird Vera and Ann. To Ann it is the most beautiful thing she has ever seen and she insists that Mom model it now. Vera makes snide remarks about Mom's large breasts. Mom puts on the nightie and I come home early by accident. I get a look at Mom without her seeing me and hurry out of the house. We have caller ID at home so I drive back to work and call from there and say I'm going to have to work late. When I get home the nightie is on the closet door and she's in her usual regular sack, asleep. Relieved, I crawl into bed beside her.

Carmine: You're afraid of me sexually.

Charley: It's because you drive me out of my mind with desire.

Carmine: Fuck you. Fuck you, Charley.

Charley: You know we were never a hot couple like that. You refused to let me touch you below the waist forever. Do you remember? It was always, 'Charley, no touching down there. You know what Mama says.'

Carmine: I buy a nice piece of lingerie hoping it will improve my husband's life and this is the thanks I get. I try to keep myself young and desirable for my miserable stinkpot of a husband and this is the kind of treatment I get.

Charley: Wear it next time the plumber comes over.

Carmine: A man like you does not deserve a woman like me.

Stories around Dad and Mom and Dad not liking sex very much are often featured, but the most poignant is my therapy episode, with Calista Flockhart as my radiant, emaciated therapist, reprising her role as Ally McBeal, who gave up her career as a lawyer to become a psychotherapist. I tell her I think sex is not so great. I tell her I never wanted to have a lot of affairs or one-night stands. She asks if I think this is normal. I tell her I think there are a lot of people who feel like I do, not much interested, but nobody listens to us; in fact, people shove sexual images at us nearly every moment of the day. By the time the episode is over we are talking about her sexual problems and she has begun to conclude that sex is maybe not all its cracked up to be. This episode, now that I think about it, was never very funny.

Ally: Is your wife interested in sex?

Charley: I don't think so. I don't see how she could be. I'm not very good at it.

Many older episodes from back in our black-and-white era are about Frank as a strange kind of son. There's the farcical episode where Frank collects fish tanks and fish and fills his room with them, every sort of fish imaginable, koi, sharks, goldfish, and a tank of piranha, his pride and joy. He feeds them strips of beef he buys himself from his part-time job helping people in the neighborhood with their computers. His prices are not cheap but this is the early era of the internet and he is in demand. He spends all his time taking care of the fish and working on people's computers. The fish episode was one of our experiments with new forms of the sitcom, very surreal, not a big hit with the audience.

"Frank Gains Thirty Pounds" is one of my favorite shows we ever did. One day I turn around and there he is, twelve years old and thirty pounds heavier. Mom says I should leave him alone, it's baby fat, it will go away. All the men in her family are big men, except for her gay brother, who is gaunt. I put Frank on a diet and we exercise together. Hilarious slapstick on the exercise equipment as the two of us get trapped on a treadmill, runaway exercise bike, one of those old fashioned steam boxes, etcetera.

Carmine: Why can't you leave my poor baby alone?

Charley: Because your poor baby is now the size of Orca the killer whale.

Carmine: Shut your mouth. What a thing to say about your own son.

Charley: To say a fact is wrong? Look at your son, Lauren.

Carmine: You know that's not my name.

Charley: (after a heavy sigh) Look at your son, Miss My-

Real-Name-is-Lauren-no-matter-how-many-times-I-tell-you-to-call-me-something-else. Look at the size of your son. Last year he could still walk through his bedroom door.

Carmine: You still hold that against him. That was a tiny door.

Charley: Last year he could still walk through it. Last year I didn't need to have a carpenter put in a bigger door.

Carmine: He gets his weight problems from you and your family.

Charley: That's great. That's incredible. Except for your brother the queer everybody in your family is the size of parade floats.

Carmine: I am not the size of a parade float.

Charley: That's only the visible part of you you're talking about. We've liposuctioned two or three extra people out of your body over the years.

Carmine: You scum.

Charley: Call me worse. What do I care? It's your son I'm talking about and you don't give a damn that he's soon going to be the size of the Hindenburg.

Carmine: You're just jealous.

Charley: I'm what?

Carmine: You're jealous because he's smarter than you and he'll go to an Ivy League school when you had to settle for a cheap public university.

Charley: Where I met you.

Carmine: Throw that in my face.

Charley: I'm jealous of Frank. That's rich.

Carmine: You're jealous of him because despite his size the girls are crazy over him and he'll have his pick.

Charley: I had my pick. Look what it got me.

Carmine: What a lovely thing to say. I've been a good wife to you.

Charley: Yes, dear. You've always been an angel.

Frank and Mom have a close relationship in which she never notices that he's swelling beyond obesity before her very eyes. She feeds him cakes and pies at Christmas and makes him sandwiches and chocolate milk when he gets home from school. Like June Cleaver, she brings her little Beaver snacks while he sits in front of his computer. He raises his prices for neighborhood computer work to the point that almost nobody hires him any more. He dresses in nothing but black and wears black eyeliner and silver earrings. Mom convinces me to buy a DSL line for the house which is really for Frank, and there's a riotously funny set of scenes in which she and I are trying to configure parental controls on the internet browser.

"Frank Gets a Date" features his snotty little sister Ann and zany Rosie from next door. He's convinced someone to go out with him and won't tell anybody who it is. Ann and Rosie speculate in wild flights of teenage fancy about who it might be. At this point, Frank is sixteen and pushing three hundred fifty pounds. We've bought him a nice outfit of clothes that are baggy and hang off him and give him a sort of watered-down gangsta look, complete with gold chains and big, multicolored running shoes. His first date is, surprisingly, a success, but we never find out who he's dating.

A theme of "Dad Is Just Too Busy" runs through script after script. Here's Dad the night Frank needs help with his application to Yale:

Frank: Dad, can you read my application essay tonight? You said you would. I have to send it off.

Charley: I'm sure it's fine.

Frank: How do you know if you haven't read it?

Charley: You're a smart boy. Why would you write a bad essay?

Frank: Don't you even care that I have a chance to get into Yale?

Charley: Yes. Of course.

Frank: My school counselor says I do.

Charley: I know you do, son. But I'm busy. I have to respond to this RFP by tomorrow. We want this job if we can get it.

Frank: You're always too busy.

Charley: It's true I'm always busy.

Frank: Fine, then. I'll just send the essay.

Charley: I'm sure it will be fine, Frankie. I'm not much of an essay writer anyway.

Frank: You could pretend to be a little interested.

His pet of the moment is a small boa constrictor that he keeps in his room. I found him in his room later with the snake around his arm trying to squeeze his hand to death.

Charley: Frank, what are you doing.

Frank: Playing with Pixie.

Charley: Get it off your arm like that. Right now.

Frank: It's not hurting me, Dad.

Charley: Is it hungry?

Frank: I don't think so. If you came in here to read the essay, it's too late. I already walked it down to the mailbox.

Charley: That's not why I came. I think you should apologize to me.

Frank: Apologize?

Charley: For interrupting my work, earlier.

Frank: Why should I apologize, Dad? I'm your son.

Charley: You upset me. I couldn't concentrate on the RFP. Now its going to take me to the wee hours of the morning.

Frank: Wow. You're serious.

Charley: It's this work I try to do that puts food on our table. Yes, I am serious.

Frank: I'm not sorry.

Charley: What?

Frank: I'm not sorry. I'm your son. I shouldn't have to be sorry for asking you a question.

Charley: That's a pretty sad attitude.

Frank: I'm not apologizing.

I nod and walk away.

This moment is indicative of the problem we always had in our family. We could never stay true to the sitcom format. Our stories were always getting too serious. We refused to give up our problems at the end of each half hour episode. We refused to resolve our lives in quick snatches of hilarity between the waves of commercials. Viewed as programming material, we were a mess.

At about age seventeen Frank was featured in a number of scripts in which he stopped speaking to me directly and referred to me in the third person. This stratagem, if I may call it that, improved interest in our series and revived our sagging ratings through his departure for college. He became a master at disdaining everything about me while keeping his hand outstretched for Yale-sized tuition and living expenses.

Charley: If you were really gifted, you'd be at Harvard.

Carmine: Charley. Please.

Frank: Tell him I don't care what he thinks. I never even applied to Harvard. I doubt he could afford for me to go there anyway.

Carmine: I'll tell him.

Charley: You were afraid to apply. Yale felt safe. To be rejected by Harvard would feel like a rebuke from the universe.

Frank: I need more money than this. This check is not big enough.

Carmine: I'll write you a check myself.

Charley: That's a laugh. When was the last time you wrote a check? Before Reagan was elected?

Carmine: I'm sure it will come back to me. It's like having sex. You never forget, no matter how long it's been. (Giving me a pointed look.)

Frank: Mom. Please.

Charley: You'll pervert his development.

Frank: Tell him to mind his own business, Mom.

Carmine: You heard your son. Mind your own business.

Charley: Does he want me to do that before or after I write him another check?

Carmine: After. Of course.

"Ann Sides with Sappho" is another classic, and the whole series that follows, while Carmine attempts to cope with her daughter's gender identity, remains one of our enduring contributions to popular entertainment. What a reality series this would have made! For days Carmine wept into her hands over the breakfast table, her breasts seeming somehow more deflated than usual, even though I knew the exact unchanging dimensions of both her implants. She lamented the grandchildren she would never have, which was, of course, a bit odd, in that by the time Ann came out to us, Frank was already married with a child well on the way. I pointed this out. It's not the same, she said. A mother bonds with her daughter during her daughter's pregnancy. It's in all the movies, she said.

Charley: Lesbians have babies.

Carmine: That's disgusting. I don't even want to talk about it.

Charley: They have to borrow somebody's sperm, of course.

Carmine: You're psycho to even talk about it. You're perverted. She probably gets this from you.

Charley: Don't put this off on me. The gay gene comes from your family, not from mine.

Carmine: Throw that in my face, too. Go ahead. My brother is gay but he's a good person and he would never have children by borrowing anybody's eggs.

Charley: Your brother would have to borrow the sperm, too.

Carmine: Oh shut up, you. You're disgusting to talk like this.

Charley: They use a turkey baster.

Carmine: A what?

Charley: Lesbians. They use a turkey baster to get pregnant. You know.

Carmine: You're sick. You're as sick as they are.

Charley: It's your daughter you're talking about. Be careful.

Carmine: You're making this up. You're sick.

Charley: No, I'm not. I saw on TV. They put a turkey baster into the sperm and stick it you-know-where. It's do-it-yourself.

Carmine: You mean they don't even use a doctor?

Charley: No. Anybody can do it. You could do it.

Carmine: At this point, that's practically what I would have to do. That's disgusting, Charley, why did you tell me that? Now I'll never get it out of my head.

Charley: So Ann could give you a whole raft full of grandchildren.

Carmine: And I'd wonder where the sperm came from for the rest of my life. The sperm of some low-life in my sweet little grandchildren.

Charley: Are you thinking about having a baby yourself?

Carmine: What, me? What are you talking about?

Charley: You just said, that was practically what you would have to do.

Carmine: I was speaking hypothetically.

Charley: That's good to know.

Carmine: Not that you would care.

Charley: Old women like you have children these days, too, you know.

Carmine: Old ladies like me? You fucking bastard.

Charley: If you could get pregnant from a vibrator you'd already have had quintuplets.

I've tried and considered various titles for our mutual family sitcom. I rejected "At Home with the Perfect Strangers" as being maybe too witty for the American public, though it's got a nice ring and I keep coming back to it. At times I've mulled over the possibility of something more straightforward, even anthropological, like "Happy Family Life." For a while I called it "Four's Company," but that seems pretty pat and there've been a dozen shows with similar titles over the years. The sitcom as a popular form is among the most banal and therefore likely among the most enduring, a kind of revival of the morality play centered on family values. My family's contribution to the form, refined into the right sequence of episodes, will have room for the kind of character development that can sustain such a series for the requisite seven to ten years, while providing its base audience with a repeat of the same comic tropes and sequences with which they long ago grew familiar. We're a sure thing, if I can ever find the time to write the scripts.

We'll want to end the series with a bang. Nothing revolutionary; we're not the type to go around pushing the boundaries of television for frivolous, selfish reasons, or even for artistic ones. We'll be content with the run-of-the-mill major ratings success that enriches everybody in sight. But we'll want to do something special for the ending. Maybe Carmine and I will get that divorce and part as old, dear friends. Maybe there'll be a horrible car accident that kills Frank, his wife, and his children, knitting the rest of the family closer together. Maybe Ann and her partner-du-jour will have triplets and move to their own chic lesbian spin-off series, "Which Mother Knows Best?"

Maybe I'll cut Carmine's throat at the end of another hilarious argument, slicing that carefully tended skin, blood sprouting all over the kitchen, and I'll lay her carefully on the new floor, some kind of fashionable tile I can't remember, from the last time we re-did the kitchen, right after I got fired.

At Last My Exclusive Interview!

BARBARA WALTERS, CHIC AND POLISHED, wearing a designer suit, expensive jewelry, is seated in an elegant armchair in my living room, beautifully lit from every angle, face conspicuously immobile, though I, an expert at paying for plastic surgery, cannot actually detect any on Barbara. Maybe a facelift? But very well done. The picture of aging gracefully, but purposeful at the moment, leaning toward me, that patented voice about to ask another question, meeting my eye so calmly, even though I am a triple murderer.

Barbara: When did you decide to kill your son and your daughter, too?

Charley: When my daughter came over to my house, caught me naked in the bathtub, accused me of abusing her, and asked me for fifty bucks to pay for a manicure.

This takes her aback for a moment, but she's a pro, she knits her brow and plunges forward.

Barbara: Did you snap? Was this some kind of mental breakdown, forced on you by the years of unemployment?

Charley: Yes. I'd had a very hard time.

Barbara: Three hundred dollars in your pocket?

Charley: One hundred.

Barbara: The mortgage past due. About to lose your house.

Charley: (Hanging my head a bit, nothing too overt) Yes. Things were about to fall apart.

Barbara: Finally, after three years of living a lie.

Charley: More like two years.

She's pausing; she's ready to follow up my earlier statement, now. She furrows that brow, considers her next question for a moment.

Barbara: Did you ever abuse your daughter?

Charley: No.

Barbara: Why would she accuse you of such a thing?

Charley: Her anorexic girlfriend put her up to it. I wasn't supposed to know they were girlfriends, either. Ann thought she had me fooled.

Barbara: Ann is your daughter.

Charley: Yes. She was.

Barbara looks me over in that classic, neutral, lips-primped way that she has. Even celebrities who thought she was their friend get that look sometimes. Martha Stewart, for instance, the night Barbara asked her whether or not she was ready to go to prison. Strip searches, group showers, Barbara leaning forward in the chair, and Martha giving a look, the shock of recognition a vampire's victim gives to a vampire, not the horror, of course, because Martha is basically fearless, but the recognition of the predator's teeth.

Barbara: Yet you say she walked in on you naked in the bathtub. Was this the first time she ever did a thing like that?

Charley: Yes.

Barbara: You never invited her to come in and watch you take a bath.

Charley: No. I never invited Ann to watch me bathe. I never abused her.

Barbara: Is that why you killed her, because she accused you?

Charley: No. I told you. I snapped.

Barbara sits back into the lamplight. At the same moment, a bit of floor-lighting comes up, to soften the shadows of her face.

Barbara: How does it feel to know so many people want you to die, Charley?

Charley: Awful. Just awful. I'm so sorry for what I've done.

Barbara: Remorseful.

Charley: Yes.

Barbara: You hoped to get away with these crimes?

Charley: (I shake my head. I'm looking at her legs. She's fit, the legs are tanned. She's obviously older but still a good looking woman.) No. I never thought I would get away with it. Not even for a moment.

Barbara: Why your son? You haven't talked much about him?

Charley: I've always hated my son.

Barbara is taken aback. Her eyebrows arch up a bit. Her tightly drawn mouth clenches a bit more. The lower part of her spine stiffens and she sits a bit straighter.

Barbara: Are you serious?

Charley: Yes.

Barbara: That seems almost. Well, almost monstrous.

Charley: Maybe hate is too strong a word.

Barbara: It's a strong word.

Charley: Dislike, then. I always disliked my son.

Barbara: Very much.

Charley: Yes. I disliked him a lot.

Barbara: Why?

Charley: He made more money than I did. Half my age and he's earning more than I am.

Barbara: You weren't earning anything.

Charley: Than I was earning the last time I was working.

Barbara: For Arthur Andersen.

Charley: Yes. I was making a lot of money then.

Barbara: But not as much as your son.

Charley: No.

Barbara: Frank.

Charley: Yes.

Barbara: Did he offer to help you when he knew you were struggling?

Charley: No. Not a word about it. He never even asked how I was getting along.

Barbara: Perhaps he disliked you, too.

Charley: What?

Barbara: Perhaps he disliked you in the same way that you disliked him.

Charley: He hated me.

Barbara: You think that's a fair word?

Charley: Yes, hate. That's the only word for it. He hated his own father.

Barbara: Had he always hated you, ever since he was a little boy?

Charley: I think so. Yes.

Barbara: Did you spend time with him? Did you take him to ball games, take him to the zoo? Did you give your son a quality part of your life?

Charley: Yes.

Barbara: You're sure of that.

Charley: Yes.

Barbara: But he disliked you anyway.

Charley: Hated me.

Barbara: According to the trial records, you were standing behind him and you attacked him without warning. You stabbed him in the chest.

Charley: Yes. I was alone in his kitchen and I got the knife.

Barbara: You had already killed your daughter.

Charley: No. I killed my son first. Then I called my daughter and told her to wait at her house till I got there, because I had a surprise for her.

Barbara: A surprise?

Charley: Yes.

Barbara: Your daughter, who claims you abused her, was willing to wait for you at her home because you were bringing her a surprise?

Charley: Actually, she didn't really accuse me of abusing her. She asked me why I hadn't. She was feeling insecure. And she was always ready for a gift.

Barbara looks at me with that well-known air of almost-not-even-there skepticism, which appears to come from the reptilian quality of her luminous eyes. I realize there is some contradiction in referring to her eyes as "reptilian" and then claiming that they are also "luminous," but Walters is a quixotic woman.

Barbara: What did you do when you got to her house?

Charley: Her roommate let me in. Her girlfriend.

Barbara: The girl you say was anorexic.

Charley: She was well known to be anorexic.

Barbara: Perhaps you don't realize it, Charley, but you're not being at all sensitive to this girl's problems.

Charley: I'm about to die, I have to tell the truth. I mean, I'm about to die when all my appeals are exhausted. Ann's girlfriend was the size of something you would use for kindling. I killed her first.

Barbara: You killed a fourth person?

Charley: Yes.

She has to think about this for a moment. No lighting change this time. She keeps her head unnaturally still. She has the same look as N— K— in the Starbucks, as if she is watching herself spin at the center of the universe.

Barbara: What was her name?

Charley: Helen.

Barbara: Hilda. Her name was Hilda.

Charley: Yes, that's right. I stabbed Hilda in the chest. She didn't even bleed. All the air went out of her and she collapsed onto the floor as this kind of filmy gauzy stuff that completely vanished without a trace. That's why there was no body.

Barbara is simply staring at the floor. She's angry, she thinks I'm making fun of her.

Charley: I'm not making fun of you.

Barbara: Let's move onto something else, shall we? You killed your daughter.

Charley: Stabbed her to death. (I am trying to feel some emotion, trying to picture Ann in the tub. Her plump, soft, white flesh soaks in the water. I open the door and she stares at me in shock. "Dad," she says, "What are you doing?")

Barbara: You loved your daughter? Her name was Laura?

Charley: Ann. Laura Annette. Yes, I loved her.

Barbara: But you're quoted as saying you were disappointed in her.

Charley: I wanted her to grow up.

Barbara: She was constantly asking you for money. Even after you lost your job.

Charley: Yes.

Barbara: Do you think you had anything to do with your daughter's apparent selfishness?

Charley: You mean, was she selfish because I was a bad father?

Barbara: Perhaps.

Charley: She was spoiled. She refused to take responsibility for herself. She had it easy and was never the least bit thankful for that. She was a lot like me, I guess.

Barbara: So you're saying yes, you were responsible. At least partially.

Charley: I thought I was a good father but I probably wasn't. I know I wasn't a good husband.

Barbara: Let's talk about your wife for a second.

I make a sound and sit back in my chair.

Barbara: Did you love your wife?

Charley: That's a very complicated question.

Barbara: Nevertheless, I'd still like you to answer it.

Charley: Yes.

Barbara: You don't say that with an enormous amount of conviction.

Charley: On the whole, I loved my wife.

Barbara: 'On the whole.' What does that mean, 'on the whole'?

Charley: When all is said and done.

Barbara: You mean, now that she's dead, you love her.

Charley: Yes.

Barbara: How did it feel to stick a knife into your wife's body? Did it make you sad?

I can feel myself tearing up. It's as if her voice, her earnestness, the smoothness of her question, and the fact that she speaks only from the center part of her lips, with the outer parts never moving, call tears out of my ducts and make me feel, all at once, the immeasurable sadness she is describing.

Charley: Yes. I feel so sad. I miss her so much.

Barbara: You feel remorse.

Charley: Yes, terrible, terrible remorse.

Barbara: Do you think your punishment is fair?

Charley: No.

Barbara: You don't?

Charley: No.

Barbara: You don't think the state should put you to death for what you did?

Charley: Absolutely not.

Barbara: What do you think should happen to you?

Charley: I think the governor should pardon me, or maybe the President should, and then I should go free, and somebody should give me a really good job.

She sits there stunned.

Charley: I've been punished enough. I have to live with what I've done for the rest of my life. I think that's enough.

Barbara: You can't be serious.

Charley: I'm perfectly serious. Look how penitent I am.

Barbara: You stabbed your wife nearly sixty times. You stabbed her in the front and then turned her over and stabbed her in the back, too.

Charley: True.

Barbara: You killed her savagely, brutally. You can't expect the Governor of xxx to pardon you and let you walk free.

Charley: My lawyer thinks there's a chance.

Barbara: Your lawyer.

Charley: Yes.

Barbara sits there for a moment, and I believe she is wishing she had some papers, some notes, in her lap, to rearrange. She looks at one of the crew behind me in an uncharacteristic fashion; for the most part she has fixed her attention on me, or on herself, in so fierce a fashion that it is as if we are completely alone. She is staring at a piece of art Carmine bought from some gallery or other.

Barbara: When your round of appeals is over and the state finally shoves that tiny lethal needle into your arm, what do you think your last words are going to be?

Charley: I don't really think it's going to come to that.

Barbara: Do you think you'll be thinking about your wife, and the terrible, terrible death you inflicted on her? Do you think she'll be uppermost in your thoughts?

In the background, a phone is beginning to ring.

Charley: That's probably the governor calling with my pardon. What do you think?

Frankly

IN THE MORNING, when I wake hung-over in my bed, my tongue feels like fungus, and my mouth is so dry my lips have cracked. I lie tangled in the sheets with a clammy feeling of sweat on my skin, wet on the outside and dry on the inside. I want to piss but at the same time I know if I move I'm going to throw up.

Last night was the night I was supposed to kill my wife. I fell asleep drunk instead.

Something is glittering on the night table in my line of vision. The bottle of potato vodka I've been drinking, nearly empty.

At the same moment that I want to reach for the vodka, the gall in my stomach rises and I know I have to get to the toilet. I lurch out of bed, my stomach churning, my lower parts wrapped in sheets, so that I stumble and hit my head on the door jamb, a good lick that smarts. I know I make some kind of groan and heave onto the tile of the bathroom floor but manage to get my head over the rim of the toilet before I let go whatever stringy bitter bile wants to come flying out of my gut. I clutch the toilet and feel my body churning, my face puffed and red, head throbbing. Most of the vomit hits the toilet but a little spatters the floor.

At some point I become conscious of voices, first the sound of the TV playing in my bedroom, something on the Turner Classic Movie channel, which has been playing all night, then another sound, real voices in the house. Maybe because I'm hung-over my hearing is acute. Carmine has company for breakfast.

I'm kneeling at the toilet soaking up the spray in wads of toilet tissue. The smell is sharp and acrid and I flush the mess away and stand, none too steadily. I got my pants off but fell asleep in my shirt and there's throw-up on the front of it, so I take it off and leave it in a heap on the floor. I find my bathrobe where I last tossed it, outside near the bed, and pull it over my arms. My skin feels cool, clammy, unhealthy. I take a swallow from the glass of tepid water by the bed.

In the kitchen sits my son, Frank. He occupies most of two chairs. He is not so much large as enormous, the size of Carmine and me put together, though impeccably dressed in a starched shirt and tailored suit, even at this hour of the morning. His hair is black as coal and gleaming, arranged in an even layer, like a cake, across his wide skull. His eyeglasses have an expensive look, thin black metal in a complex boxy-ovoid shape. To my knowledge there is nothing wrong with his eyes; he began wearing fake eyeglasses in college to make himself look more serious in class, about the same time he stopped dressing like a gangsta. He wears the best silk tie two hundred dollars can buy. He drips affluence even when he is not dripping sweat due to his bulk, nearing four hundred pounds by this point. Chins hang from his jaw like veils. He gives me a sharp, hard look.

Carmine, completely dressed, is leaning against the granite countertop near the stainless steel juicer. "You're awake."

"Yes. Did you make coffee?"

"What's to make? I turn on the machine and press a button. If you want a cup, push the button for yourself."

I say to Frank, "This is what I get from her. She won't even so much as push a button on my behalf."

"You're starting a little early this morning, Dad."

I blink at him, and look from him to her. "What do you mean?"

"You're drunk."

"If I'm a little drunk it's from last night."

"He never sobers up any more," Carmine says. "It's like living with a pickle."

Frank is clutching a lilac colored handkerchief in his stubby fingers. I expect the handkerchief came with the suit. Frank uses it to wipe his forehead. "Won't that be a problem when you head off for your job interview thing this morning? Oh. That's right. You don't have one." Frank's expression and voice brim over with disdain. His voice grates on my skin. "Man. You look like a wreck."

"You want to know what you look like, Frankie?" I ask.

He blinks at me.

"You want to know what you look like, spread out there like a pond?"

"Leave him alone," Carmine says.

"You look like twins, stuffed into one shirt," I say. "So don't tell me I look like a wreck when there you are."

His eyes narrow. His lips thin. A father who has ever had any hold over his son can always score a hit. Frankie and I were friends when he was young.

"He's over here trying to help us," Carmine says, her voice raised.

At that point, I note that Frankie's meaty pink hand is resting on a fair-sized pile of envelopes. I see my name on one.

"What are you doing with my mail?" I ask.

"Opening it," Frankie says. "Which is more than you've done in weeks. Months."

"How dare you? You have no business in my office for any reason."

"I invited him," Carmine says, "blame me."

She is watching her son, her Frankie, with the most complete tenderness. I envy him for a moment, that he can call such moist feelings out of her.

"You're losing the house," Frankie says. He laces finger through finger and sits there with his hands smugly arranged, waiting.

My head starts to pound. "We're what?"

"You're losing the house. The bank is foreclosing. Here are your notices from the bank's agent. You haven't even bothered to open them."

Carmine is staring at the floor. She flicks something out of one eye and draws a long, ragged breath. Her forehead and dimples no longer move due to Botox. She is making something like one-third to one-half of a facial expression. I feel the first tug of sympathy I've had for her in days.

"Dad," says Frank, in that petite, high-pitched voice of his; the voice of a smaller person, whom I sometimes think Frank swallowed and is holding captive. "Are you with me?"

"Yes."

"These notices are about the bank calling in your loan. You got them weeks and weeks ago."

"I thought they were bank statements. I don't open bank statements."

"What are you talking about, they don't even look like bank statements. They don't even come in the same kind of envelope." He sets his fake glasses on the table. His wife Ramona says they make his face look smaller. "Mom and I are going to see an attorney this morning."

My heart is pounding. I feel dry in the mouth, as if I've grown a desert on my tongue.

He hands me a letter and I stare at it. It's from some county court or other, summoning me to come and explain why the bank should not call in the loan and take back the house.

"Can you pay what's due?" Frank asks. "At this meeting with the court?"

I fold the letter and feel my heart pounding. It's over now. I'm clammy with sweat, but it's over, and there's a certain amount of relief involved. "They'll want the whole loan, Frank. You know that."

"But you could offer to pay what we owe," Carmine says.

I ignore her, my eyes on my son. "You're a banker, Frankie. You know how this works."

"No, I don't," he says. "I don't work with home mortgages. I work with a whole different side of the bank."

"Don't kid me you don't know this. They want the whole loan when they call it in. That's all they'll take."

"You can't even pay the arrears, can you? You don't have the money." That's the question he really wants answered. That's why he was asking in the first place.

I run my hand along my scalp, searching for the wispy hairs. One of my new annoying habits is to tug these wispy hairs on the top of my head and at the back of my neck, and I bend my head and start to do that. The letter from the court is sitting in my hand.

"You had to have known you weren't paying the mortgage," Carmine says.

"Right," Frank says, touching his own black hair, thinning at the crown, looking at me. "What are you doing?"

"Plucking at my hair."

"It's his new habit," Carmine says. "He does it all day."

"How much money do you have left, Dad?"

"Your mother doesn't tell you?"

"My mother doesn't know."

"Has she tried to use her ATM card today?"

Frank looks at her. She says, "The card's not working. I need a new one."

This is that part of a murder which detective shows leave out, even the best of them. Preceding the murder, there's a long, messy, savage kind of scene shared among a few people who will participate in the final drama. I can feel it beginning, the wave of rage, when she says this stupid line about the ATM.

"The machine doesn't give her money so the card's not working," I say to Frank.

He tries to bury his head in his hands but it's too big and his hands are small, almost petite, in comparison. Carmine is looking at the floor. "The card's supposed to give me money so how am I supposed to know why it doesn't?"

"Mother, calm down."

"What does he mean? What does your father mean?" It's beginning to dawn on her.

"Your card's working fine, Mom," Frank says.

"We don't have any money," I say. "It's gone."

She sips her coffee. A drop spills on her skirt, a single, tiny drop, that nobody sees but me. Her hand is shaking. "That can't be true."

"I took out the last cash yesterday," I said.

"All of it?"

I chuckle. "That's right. The whole hundred dollars."

She's in a sudden spitting rage. "That can't be true. You must think I'm crazy." There's something ridiculous about her fury given that at least thirty percent of her face remains completely motionless no matter what. "There's got to be some account."

"Did I ever get a cup of coffee?" I ask.

"Here," she says, and hands it to me from the counter. I don't remember getting the cup or pressing the button on the coffee robot. I take the cup and sip. It's cold. "Did you hear me?"

The coffee disagrees with my stomach right away and I put it down. I'm feeling bloated, like I'll need to fart in a minute. There's no way to do that in these stainless steel chairs of Carmine's without making some kind of sound.

"Charley, did you hear me?"

"Yes. I heard you. There's no account."

"Don't you have any CDs?"

"Mom, nobody has CDs any more," Frank says. He's shuffling through the stack of envelopes, bright red to the ears.

"We have to find some money somewhere," Carmine says, "I can't just lose my house."

"The stocks are gone. Our annuities are gone. The cash I got paid for losing my wonderful job is gone."

"We can sell the cars," Carmine says.

"You think I've been paying off the car loans if I haven't been paying the mortgage?"

She stands from the counter, turning her back on me. She's trembling.

"It wouldn't do any good anyway, Mom."

"What do you mean, we haven't even asked anybody. We haven't even spoken to anybody at the bank."

"Like Dad said. They've called in the loan."

"What does that mean, they've called it in? Can they do that?"

"It means they want payment for the whole loan amount. They can do that when you're delinquent, yes."

"Nobody ever told me that."

"You signed a contract when you bought the house."

"I never signed any paper that said they could take my house like this. We've paid on this house for years, they can't just take it."

"You did sign a paper like that, Ma."

"I never."

His face purples; he raises his voice and speaks emphatically. "You did." He slaps his hand on the table again. He mops with the handkerchief. Rolls of him are unsettled all the way down to his lower ribs.

"Don't shout at me."

"I wouldn't have to shout at you if you'd listen."

"Don't talk to me like this, Frankie. It's bad enough with your father." She is silent for a moment, watching him. "So what happens now?"

"The court sells the house. Auctions it." His face is running with sweat. He puts down the coffee, which he has been holding against his immaculate shirt just under his chin, without spilling a single drop on the shirt.

"How can there not be any money?" Carmine turns to me, parts of her face turning pale under her spray tan. She's fumbling through her Prada purse for gum. Designer gum from a health food store, no sugar, no additives, no flavor at all. It's called, "Just Gum." I think they make it out of tofu. "How could we run out of money? You've only been out of a job for two years."

I glare at her. "So now it's two years. Yesterday it was three. So when it's to your advantage, you add on the extra year?"

She refuses to be derailed. "How could we run out of money? How could we spend all that money?"

"You never even had a plan, did you?" Frank speaks into

the palms of his hands. He's leaning on the table, this morning's *USA Today* under his arm. "You never so much as did a budget."

"Yes I did."

"When?"

"Do I answer to you?"

"Yes, Dad, you answer to me."

"Since when?"

"Since the county decided to auction your house for you."

I get up and pull the robe together. I have an image of myself, hair grizzled and tufted out from where I've been plucking at it, white T-shirt grimy because I'm not sure what day I put it on or what pile it was in when I found it, boxers clean but so baggy over the sticks of my legs that I look like some kind of bizarre walking water balloon. My calves are shiny and bald. Black socks that I fell asleep in are bunched around my ankles, only one of the socks is actually navy blue, and I've slid my feet into my wife's purple fuzzy half-slipper flip-flop bedroom shoes. My knees knob out like on an old pioneer door.

"Where are you going?"

"I need to use the toilet."

"Use the one right here," Carmine says, "Deutze put fresh paper in there yesterday."

"Deutze always puts fresh paper in there."

"So rub it in that you love Deutze so much," she shouts. She's managed a tear now, and pulls back her hair to make sure we see it. "Rub it in that you want to screw the maid on top of losing the house."

"You brought her up," I say.

Frank is coming to a boil. "Look after your son," I say, "he's about to pop."

There's no peace in the bathroom with the two of them

whispering just down the hall. I look through a copy of *Architectural Digest* where a couple has built a stunning modern house with all white walls and the usual magnificent window forty feet high. They're standing arm-in-arm in the middle of the vaulted room like two snuggly stuffed animals, looking proudly at all their objects. Carved space. Crap. Looks like the atrium of a mall. I wash my hands and flush the toilet. The smell of my guts must be pretty putrid, I think, if this is any evidence. I wrap the robe around me and amble out to the hall again.

I'm walking like a seventy-year-old man. I'm walking like my father at seventy, with his gouty knees and arthritis, shuffling across the old dining room rug for a glass of milk.

"Yes, I made a budget," I say, sitting down in the chair with a huff. The stainless steel has lost all the warmth it gathered from my butt and starts leeching more. "But this is your mother, who couldn't any more live on a budget than walk to the hair parlor."

"That's ten miles from here," she says, "I drive all the way across town. You know that."

"To the corner store, then. Couldn't walk to the corner store."

"I could live on a budget. I did when I was in college."

I laugh and then feel nauseous and hold my head between my knees.

"Are you all right?" she asks. "Do you need a glass of water?"

"That would be nice."

"The glasses are next to the refrigerator," she says.

"For Christ's sake, mother." Frank grips the back of the chair and the edge of the table fiercely and heaves himself to his feet. He's still pretty mobile once he's up on his feet, and according to his wife he takes her dancing on occasion at a country club they joined. He can get through a polka and a half before he has to sit down. He fills me a glass of water from the chilled tap at the front of the stainless steel refrigerator.

"Thank you, son," I said. The cold water is soothing and I put the glass against my forehead.

"Smell from the bathroom," Carmine says, waving her hand. "Pew. There's spray right in there, Charley. Every time you go in there I tell you to use it and you never do."

"I can't sit here all day," Frankie says. "What are you going to do?"

"Why are you worried?" I ask. "Your mother is divorcing me anyway."

"Throw that in my face," she says. Adding another stick of "Just Gum" to the one in her mouth.

"You should have a lot of equity in the house," Frankie says.

"There's a line of credit."

"What's that?" Carmine's voice is slightly blurred by the gum. Twenty years ago she would have been smoking cigarette after cigarette. Now it's the gum.

"We borrowed money against our equity in the house."

"That's a good thing, right? You told me it was good when we did it."

"It was cheap money. That's what I told you."

"You told me it was a good thing. And now what? They want us to pay that back, too?"

"Yes, Mother," Frank snapped. "It's a pretty basic principle. When you borrow money they want you to pay it back."

"Don't talk to me like that."

"You're acting so fucking stupid, Mother."

"Charley, tell your son not to use that kind of language. Why do we have to pay it back now? That's all I mean."

He takes a moment and literally hisses, at a low level, like a hum. Rubbing his forehead in both small hands, he swirls the last of his coffee in the cup.

"I'll make you another," Carmine says, and takes the cup.

"The equity loan is secured against the house," Frankie says. "If the court sells the house you have to pay the equity loan back, too."

"She knows that. She's not stupid."

"I did not know that." The coffee robot is grinding the beans and heating the water and spits out another cup. "That's lousy planning. That's terrible planning."

"That's not something you can plan, mother. That's the way equity loans work."

"This is what I mean about a budget," I say. "This woman could not live on a budget for the length of time it takes to piss on one."

"You never made any such budget, Charley, and yes, I could live on one. I could live on a budget a lot faster than you could, you house-losing bastard."

"You think I showed it to you? Why would I show a budget to you? It has numbers on it. You don't deal with numbers. How many times have you told me that?"

"I've heard you say that at least a thousand times, Ma," Frankie says.

"Anything with numbers was your father's responsibility."

I laugh quietly. Frankie heaps six spoons of sugar into his coffee and stirs it. He puts the cup in the microwave to get it hotter. This requires his getting up again, a ponderous process. He stands back from the microwave by the five or six feet that his mother has always required, in order to save his brain from turning into radioactive goo. He takes the heated coffee and pours cream into it and sits down again.

I sit there and stare at my son's knees, dimpled and wide, in the fabric of the tailored suit.

In daylight the kitchen is a bright room, facing the back yard, where we can look out through the sun room to the pool and the privacy fence. Now there's a gray, early morning quality to the light.

"Should I make breakfast?" Carmine asks. "Is anybody hungry?"

Frankie is watching me. For a moment he has no hostility in his eyes, and he actually sees me, looks at me. In that face right now is a person I used to know, a boy who used to let me play with him in his He-Man Castle, who occasionally shared his favorite Transformers with me. Most of the time I was too busy screwing up another hospital billing system to play but sometimes I said yes. I would pretend I didn't know how to transform the Transformer and he would show me with the cutest seriousness. That child is still here, still wishing for something. "You know you've gotten yourself into a mess that I can't get you out of."

The finality of it comes down on me. It's all the relief in the world to know.

"What do you mean?" Carmine asks. "Where will we go?"

"Where were you going to go when you were divorcing me?"

"I'm still divorcing you, you bastard."

"Well," I say, spreading my hands generously, "now you know what you're going to get out of it."

Tears are streaming down Carmine's face. Most of the face is trembling. "I don't understand how you could let this happen."

"You must have known you were in trouble, Dad. You let all this mail pile up. You must have known."

I blow out a breath as much like a fart as I can make it.

Frank starts to shove himself up from the chair and decides against it. The TV alarm goes off on the kitchen counter and Katie Couric says, "Back to you, Matt." Carmine reaches for the off-button automatically. "I wish I could figure out who the hell set this alarm. I can't figure out how to turn it off."

"I'll get my son to reset it when he comes over," Frank said. "He figured out our VCR."

"Every living morning I come in here for coffee and there's fucking Katie Couric on the fucking *Today* show."

"Watch your mouth," I say.

"You'll probably have to sell that TV anyway. It's a plasma screen, you can get some money for it."

That freezes Carmine, and disturbs me. The losses won't stop with the house, of course, Frank's right. He's usually right when he's blunt like that and the subject concerns money. Carmine is rubbing the corner of the TV like she wants to convince a genie to come out of it.

"We never should have spent that kind of money on a TV," she says, she who saw a flat screen plasma TV about this size in her friend Rhonda Blakeley's kitchen and had to have one, yes, that very weekend. because she heard there was a sale at Best Buy.

"I told your father we didn't need a TV in the kitchen but he had to have it. These flat screen things cost so much money."

"You were the one who wanted it. Miss I-Might-Want-To-Make-A-Soufflé-Someday."

"You're such a liar, Charley." She tosses her head exactly as if she's putting a cigarette to her lips.

"The same way you wanted the fifteen-hundred-dollar coffee robot, and the nine-hundred-dollar juicer. When was there ever a piece of fruit in this kitchen? When did I ever eat a piece of fruit?"

"I eat fruit."

"You can't even name one."

"I eat tomatoes."

"That's not a fruit."

"Yes it is."

"All right, you eat tomatoes. Did you ever once make nine hundred dollars worth of tomato juice in the juicer?"

She bites off half of her gum and throws it in the stainless steel garbage can. "Don't change the subject to me. You could have told me we were running out of money, you rat bastard."

"For twenty years I was lucky enough to earn more money than you spent. When did I once ever please even once convince you not to buy a single thing?"

"We always had money then."

"You knew I was out of work. Did it never occur to you there was a bottom we were going to hit sooner or later?"

"So it's me. It's all me. I wasn't sensitive enough when you lost your job."

"How sensitive do you need to be to decide not to redo the kitchen for thirty thousand dollars? For the second time redo the kitchen, I mean. Forgive me. How sensitive do you need to be to decide that it's a bad idea to redo the kitchen when your husband is out of work?"

"We thought you were going to get another job right away."

"I never thought that. There were no jobs."

"We both wanted to redo the kitchen, we talked about it."

"It was a recession. There were no jobs."

"Your friends got jobs."

"Stop with this already, you said it a thousand times."

"You could have taken any job, anything, to bring in some money."

"What about you?" I ask.

She sits there with a compact searching her face to see if it shows that she's been crying. The light's not good so she moves the mirror and her head this way and that.

"Why is it me that's supposed to get my brains blown out working on the night shift in some fucking 7-11?" I ask.

She touches a tissue to the corner of her mouth like it's a frigging science experiment, like she's some kind of surgeon.

Frank heaves to his feet. This time he uses no hands at all. "The two of you are priceless."

"What, Frankie? Where are you going?"

"Out for some air."

"The doors by the pool are open already, sweetie," Carmine says. "Sit in the chair right there. You'll get a good breeze."

"What time is the lawyer appointment?"

"Ten o'clock."

"Why did you get me over here so early, then?" Frank asks, red-faced, from the poolside door. I can see him across the eating bar.

"Because I thought you and your father would need to go through accounts and things."

"I could have been in bed another hour."

"Don't be upset with me, Frankie. My nerves can't take it."

"Your nerves have got to go," Frankie says. "Your fucking nerves are running me ragged."

"Watch your mouth."

"You said 'fuck' yourself not ten minutes ago. Didn't she, Dad?"

"She's always had a foul mouth when you kids weren't around," I say. "I've put up with her abuse for years."

She flings the Prada bag at my head. It's pretty light

since most of the contents are strewn on the counter at the moment. I deflect it and it slides on the floor. It's one of her old Prada bags; she must have filled it for show, knowing she'd want to hurl it at some point. She's picking up one prescription bottle after another.

"You seeing your divorce attorney? That who you're seeing?"

"No. We're seeing somebody Frankie knows who does real estate. But don't worry. I plan to see my divorce attorney as soon as I find one."

"How you going to pay for him? or her? or whatever?"

She looks at me as if this is a completely new thought. She's frozen, transfixed. Parts of her face are even more motionless than usual.

"We should sell all this crap in the house," I say. "We'll get some cash for it. Get rid of some of our clothes."

"Shut up, Charley."

"I'm talking to myself now. I can sell my suits used. You don't need nice Italian suits if you're working at a convenience store."

"You pisser," she says. Now that Frankie's not in the room she gives up the teary eyes. "You lose everything we have and you act like it's nothing."

A knot of something hard forms in my stomach with her face making this expression that I hate, that I loathe, this blind denial of everything we've been talking about for the last hour, this twisting of the whole conversation to a summary that will make me look as bad as possible. With us a conversation is never about talking, it's about winning. "How am I supposed to talk to you?" I ask.

"You open your mouth and talk, just like usual."

"You never listen."

"I never listen? Here is the king of not listening telling me that I never listen."

"I am not the one who lost our money. We lost it. You and me together. Don't you get that?"

"The numbers were your job, Charley. The money was your job. It was always your job."

"Why is it that my job was always whatever you said it was? Why is it I never got a choice?"

"You got a choice, Charley, you married me. After that, there was no choice."

"Amen to that."

"So you lost all our money and our house and our cars and you want to get in my face about where I'm going to live and what I'm going to do?" She's shaking now, shoving her stuff by the handful back into the purse she threw at me. "If you needed me to change all you had to do was ask. We could have sold the house and moved to someplace smaller. We could have sold the cars and just had one apiece. There are so many things we could have done."

"Six months ago I asked you about selling the house. Do you remember?"

"You weren't serious."

The fact that she says this makes me boil but I contain it and take a breath. "That was the first time you brought up divorce. Do you remember?"

She closes the bag with effort. "We weren't serious. We were joking around."

"I was serious, Carmine."

"No, you weren't."

"You see? This is what it's like trying to talk to you. I never know what you heard till you repeat it back to me later, and it's never what I remember. You don't even live in the same world as I do."

She gives me a poison smile. "That's right, Charley. I live in the world where men pay the mortgage on time and talk to their wives about their problems. You never heard of that world."

"That's a great world for you," I say. "It fucks me completely. But what do you care?"

"I don't even know what you're talking about."

"All I want is once in your life for you to admit that you might have done something wrong. That you might have been part of the problem."

"Sure I did things wrong," she says, again with that cigarette gesture. "But I was a good wife to you and a good mother to your children and I kept up my part of the bargain."

My head is pounding. "I can't get through to you."

"Our marriage was a mistake from the start," she says. "I never should have married a man with such a low level of passion."

"What are you talking about? Now it's my passion that's the problem?"

"You never liked sex, Charley."

I'm breathless. She sees it. Her opening.

"You never liked making love to me. I deserve better. I deserve more passion."

"Neither one of us was ever that passionate. Neither one of us."

"I always felt like I was missing something from you. But I settled for it anyway because you were so comfortable."

"Sex isn't the whole fucking world, Carmine. You didn't like it any better than I did."

She takes a complacent breath. "I might have. If I'd been with the right person."

The case is made in her head now. She has her facts lined up the way she wants them. Nothing I can say will ever change that.

I'm finished talking. A knot of something hard in me. I can still do something with my life, but it won't be pretty.

"You should talk to that lawyer about personal bankruptcy," I say. "Don't waste your time about the house."

"That's a good idea," she says, and looks at me coldly. "Maybe I'll get a referral for a good divorce lawyer, too."

I laugh. "Threaten me with that. Go ahead. I'm ready for the divorce now. I'm so ready I'm dancing all over the house. You'll get nothing from me. We have nothing left to fight over."

"I'll find something," she says, her eyes as hard as glass.

She walks into the sunroom with Frankie.

There is a rack of knives across the kitchen, very expensive Japanese cutlery, sharpened to a turn, kept there in case some itinerant gourmet wanders through the neighborhood and offers to cook for us some night.

The moment with Carmine is over. Out of this wreck will come the story of bad Charley and how he failed at everything, marriage, work, and manhood. From the ashes will emerge blameless Carmine thrown on the mercy of the whims of the world. That is a role Meg Ryan could have played, but it's Joan Crawford I see across the house, standing with her arm on my son.

I get a bottle of bourbon from the bar, pour a long shot in a glass, swallow most of it, pour more and take another gulp. Warmth spreads through me. I'm sill alive.

I stand at the rack of knives.

Frankie will be too slow to save her.

I'll have to kill him, too. I've thought about it. I should probably do him first. But now, when it comes right down to it, can I?

It's These Geese Again

I DREAM I'M IN BED WITH Tom Cruise and
Vanessa Redgrave. The other Redgrave whose name I can
never remember is in the bathroom and won't come out.
She is passing a lot of gas in the bathroom. Vanessa and
Tom are talking about where to go for breakfast. I'm feeling
sweaty and wet. I'm looking at a book of pictures. It looks
like a Dr. Seuss book about two gay boys and a cat. I can
read the Dr. Seuss rhymes and hear them very clearly in
my head and the writing sounds exactly like him. Two gay
boys have a cat, a green cheese, and a purple onion. There
is no good rhyme for onion, maybe bunion, which is not
necessarily a good word for a poem, so it can't be an onion.
This is passing through my mind at the time and the story
therefore changes while I'm reading it. I never see Tom and
Vanessa doing anything, I only see them lying together in

their robes. They have the same luminous skin tone. "There go those geese again," she says at one point, and Tom looks where she indicates, and they nod.

Someone models a pair of jeans for me, a bony teenager with dark eye makeup, walking hands on hips, new jeans that look like they've been pounded on a rock for days by a jean-pounding machine. Hugging her hips low, the pants are always crawling lower, and she pulls them up and tugs at the hem of her blouse. She is cool as ice except when she's tugging her shirt down or her pants up.

I think for the first time that I am probably dreaming but the thought passes and Tom hands me a cup of something. Coffee, but I can't smell it. A supplement to aid my aging memory is in the cup, Vanessa says. "You'll remember every-thing now," she says.

"All the time?"

"Yes. I think so."

Wouldn't that be pleasant! I sip it and it has a sticky creamy taste, like medicine.

"It's not coffee."

"It's better than coffee." Tom smiles. "I promise."

"It's sticky."

"So it will be good for your eyes," Tom says.

We are in a car and Tom is driving and I am in the back seat wrapped in the blankets. They understand that I was still dreaming before and therefore still sleeping and that I probably need to do more of that, so I lie down. We are driving through Wyoming headed toward the mountains. Outside the SUV is very cold. Tom left the road long ago and we're crossing rough country.

"It's those geese again," Vanessa says, and points.

"There they go," Tom says.

I look for the geese and the blanket falls away from my shoulder and I'm cold.

The SUV gets stuck in a rock. No one thinks it's acci-
dental for a car to get stuck in a boulder like that, and no
one, including Tom, knows how it happened. He says he
was driving like always. Then Vanessa said look out for the
rock. Vanessa agrees that she said that. She does not remember seeing a rock, but she remembers saying look out for
one. After that everybody gets out of the SUV and looks at
the boulder with the car stuck in it. About half of the front
is gone, vanished inside the rock. Vanessa says she doesn't
think it's even possible. Tom says he only looked away for a
second and bam! We're going to have to camp out here until
someone comes, Vanessa says.

"I'll sleep in the back seat," I say. "My blanket's already
there, and it's not stuck in the rock."

They agree. They make a pile of things on the ground.

I want to open my eyes but I can't. The lids are so heavy.
I feel like I'm lying on a couch. It feels more like a couch
than it does the back seat of an SUV.

"Did he kill his wife?" Vanessa asks.

"No, I don't think so."

We've already lost the house, I think. The court has
already sold it. That's why I'm sleeping in a car.

Vanessa says, "I really didn't think he would. Not murder."

"He might have, except that his son was there."

"I don't think he'd have done it anyway."

"You're wrong, he definitely would have. He doesn't feel
anything for his wife. A big lump of nothing is what he
feels."

"That's a far cry from hacking her up. From what I hear,
he never even cut up a chicken."

Tom laughs. "He's not cutting her up, he's killing her and
leaving her there."

"Still."

"If a man is angry enough."

"What if a woman is angry? What can she do?"

"I don't even need to know that," Tom says, shaking his head.

"A woman can't do anything."

"I think he would have picked up that knife in another second or so," Tom said. "If the phone hadn't rung."

Geese are crying, a wing of them flying across the sky, I see it from upside down in the van. I want to tell the others, but I don't know how.

It still feels like I'm lying on a couch. We're all outside and it's cold now. We should go back to the van. I think I'm naked. They'll notice in a minute. I have the blankets in the van, why didn't I bring them out? The light's so bright out here. Where is the couch, anyway? The light is getting brighter. I'm sure I'm naked now, and everybody is going to look at me, and they do, and see, and then my eyes are open and I'm awake.

I'M LYING ON THE COUCH in the family room, some kind of blanket wrapped around me. I'm cold. I've been cold for a while.

The house is quiet.

I sit up. I am drunk again, buzzing, still queasy. My arm hurts near the shoulder, there are fresh scabs there. My head throbs from where I fell in the bathroom.

I'm naked under the blanket. How did I get on the couch?

Carmine and Frank are gone, no voices from the kitchen. They must have left for the attorney's office. Maybe one of them walked me to the couch.

The room is peaceful. Morning light falls through the shutters, bright bars on the window, in the air, on the floor. In this room Carmine's choice of objects is at its best; the sectional couch is long and comfortable, easy to burrow into, without an excess of pillows; the tables and chairs are simple modern stuff from Sweden, clean lines made of glowing wood; the entertainment center is silent at the moment, the wide dark screen inviting, as if I could climb into the murk and stay. Thick white carpet and scattered rugs in some kind of abstract art design. An indoor palm and a huge philodendron sit in handmade pots by the wide windows.

There's a sweet smell in the air, not like anything I remember.

On the floor in the doorway to the kitchen lies someone's hand. Carmine's hand sprawls open on the linoleum with her wedding ring and engagement ring showing. Red tracery twines over the fingers and back of the hand and disappears out of sight along the wrist; I can't see any more because of the door, until I lurch up from the couch.

She is lying in the kitchen on her back. There's a phone handset a few feet away, nearer to her feet. She's stabbed in the face, in the neck, in the back, from the torso up. A terrible wound splits her throat and a pool of dark blood cools on the floor. A slash across the face peeled off part of her cheek. She smells like a toilet; her dress is soiled.

On the kitchen counter sits a bottle of bourbon with a glass beside it, a couple of fingers of bourbon in the glass, only a little more than that in the bottle.

Beyond, in the sunroom beside the doors to the pool, lies Frank, chair overturned on its back and him still sitting in it, one leg slid off the seat to the side, leaning against the glass of the window. His shirt is covered with blood. His throat is cut, and a large dark puddle has spread around him. His mouth is open and a fly is crawling on it.

I get sick looking at him and heave on the carpet, breaking into a sweat. Somewhere inside me there should be a deep pain from this, because he looks like my little boy again. His face is angelically pale and clear. There are no wounds on it. His eyes are open. He appears to be staring into a movie playing just above his head in the air. At moments I think I can see him breathing.

Did I kill her mother, too, did I kill Carmine's mother?

She's in her room on the other side of the house, sleeping peacefully, face mask over her eyes. If she took her usual snort and a sleeping pill, she could be out for a while.

My robe is next to Carmine on the kitchen floor, soaked with blood. It's torn. Should I take it?

There's a knife next to the sink, washed clean. The blade is keen, a long blade, what my mother would have called a butcher knife.

In my room I grab a bag and shove some clothes in it. I pull on a running suit and clean underwear, smelling myself. There's a spot of blood on my bare foot. I get my son's wallet. He carries it in the inner pocket of his jacket, which is hanging on the back of the chair in the kitchen; I don't have to go near any of his blood, and I step carefully around Carmine. His car keys are there, too, and I take them.

I put the knife in my bag at the last minute, just before leaving the house.

Movie Nature: A Flashback

MOVIE PEOPLE SOLVE their problems by violence. To be a movie person, that is, a person whose story might be told in the movies, I had to solve my problem the same way.

Violence is an expression of both good and evil in the movie world; evil by its nature erupts into violence and good must resort to violence to tame evil.

My marriage to Carmine could only have been reconciled in a small, independent film; we never had a blockbuster marriage to begin with, so a story centered on its preservation would never have generated much buzz. To achieve blockbuster status one of us had to die. Since I was playing the role of killer, Carmine's role was therefore clear.

Carmine had walked into the sunroom to talk to Frank

and then walked through the open doors outside. I was warm from the deep swig of bourbon and stood touching the keen edge of the knife to the tips of my fingers.

I drank more bourbon and walked directly around the table behind Frank. He was angry at me and ignoring me and never suspected a thing. Even then I knew better than to hesitate when I stood behind him, looking into his moussed, thinning hair.

I cut his throat while Carmine stood outside looking at the pool, the heavy knife easing through the white skin and flesh and biting deep, blood in gushes; I pulled the blade against him hard till his windpipe severed. He convulsed and tried to turn his head and his arms splayed out in a spasm. He made this harsh barking sound and his limbs went rigid, maybe with panic. My heart was pounding but any feeling other than rage was distant. All I could see was what I had to do to kill Carmine, and getting rid of Frankie was the first step. Blood streamed down the front of his suit. From behind I pulled his chair onto the tile with his throat spurting, his arms flopping down, one heavy leg sliding against the table, but no struggle or fight. I refused to look anywhere near his eyes, but I could see a spasm cross his lips, blood at the corner. Suddenly I was a strong man, not old at all, and I stabbed him deep in the chest twice. He made more gurgling noise out of his windpipe, loud.

The narrative always implies an implicit right for the killer to kill, because the narrative thrives on killing. In my mind there is only one course of action left, and therefore my brain closes off all others, and all objections. The narrative constricts itself to a focused frame and I see only what comes into the frame. The consequences of my actions are a later scene, maybe never to be written or filmed.

We think like the movies. What we don't see or don't

believe or don't agree with falls out of the frame. What is left in the picture is what we want to see, the movie that moves us most. Each of us sees the movie separately, and what I see in the movie never coincides with what another sees. I make a movie in which I must kill Carmine, and when the moment comes it is the only choice left to me. It is the only choice left functioning in my mind; all the other choices have surrendered, and I pick up the knife.

Carmine maybe heard the sound of me wrestling Frank and the chair onto the floor and turned, but by the time she realized what had happened I had her by the hair and pulled her inside. She grabbed the knife but instead of screaming started hissing at me like this was a fight she meant to win. I punched her hard in the stomach and then kicked her and she fell to her knees and I stabbed her in the back as deep as I could and then did it again. I wasn't saying anything and she was gasping and these other, strange sounds were coming out of Frank and from Carmine too, and a foul smell came over the room from Frank and I was enraged and stabbed her really hard and slashed her across the face with her eyes looking right at me. I never felt such hate for anything. Where it came from I don't know. I never felt like that about her before, not that intense. She was trying to say something and I tried to slice her mouth and then got behind her and cut her throat. A spray of blood went out across the floor and she lay in it. She was moving as if some kind of current were in her and so I stabbed her in the back once more, leaning on the blade to drive it in deep. After a few minutes she got still and I took out the knife. We were in the kitchen by then. She had pulled off my robe and used her fingernails on my arm; she dug in pretty deep, fighting for her life; two of the nails were broken and my arm was burning and bleeding.

I killed Carmine to cross a line. To find a higher self. It is the choice one sees made in a movie, so clearly, when the action hero blows away the first of the thugs. He sets his jaw and cocks his gun from his hip and does his duty. He has the power of judgment. He is law and order wrapped up in one flesh. The only reality is to be his friend or his enemy and I can never be his friend, I can never be man enough for that.

With malice aforethought, I wreck our finances, lose our house, ruin our marriage, and kill Carmine, in order to create a moral dilemma. Without a moral dilemma at which to succeed or fail, what am I? I can't remember ever thinking of myself as a hero. But I have a mighty failure in me, and I give it everything I have.

Villains are remembered among movie people, often as fondly as heroines or heroes or even more so.

Murdered wives are portrayed more vividly than faithful ones. Murdered and unfaithful wives are very near the top of the heap in terms of status, thinking of Anna Karenina as a murdered wife (though she murdered herself, of course), or Marilyn Monroe as Rose Loomis in *Niagara* (who also murdered herself, but in real life), or Rebecca DeWinter, for whom a priceless mansion burns. Though I know she would never thank me, I have given Carmine, in memory, a longer life than she would have had in years.

What should my ending be? A strong man who loved his family but killed them in a fit of drunken rage would put a pistol to his own head or find some other painful way of dying. A wicked weasel of a man would fight to go on living, to be proven innocent of his murders, to seek support from his daughter whom he did not kill, to beg forgiveness on his hands and knees. A slimy, evil, shadow of a human being would try to escape prison and punishment with every trick and lie he can think of. Temporary insanity. Had just learned I lost my house. Wife accusing me of sleeping with the maid, of being impotent, of never satisfying her in bed. Pushed over the edge. Already drunk and my wife knew it. Flew into a rage and grabbed the knife. Manslaughter, not murder. I never premeditated a thing.

A good man, a man who was killing only out of rage, would have killed his wife first and left his son alone. A wicked man, a worthless man, a failure of a human being would kill his son first so that the son would not prevent the killing of the wife. Both kinds of men are indispensable to storytelling.

The power of evil is its power to transform in narratively interesting ways, and for this reason evil is vital to movie nature. Good is not vital, good can only transform at the end, because once goodness triumphs, there is no more story. A person's life is transformed by some evil moment, choice, or accident, and thereafter the life is stronger, more defined and clear. The transformations brought about by goodness are rarely as dynamic and are useful only for the background of stories, the time that has passed or is coming to an end, or the time that is about to be.

In movies, evil may never be finally vanquished in order that violence may always have a purpose. Stars are born in violence. Only by violence might I also become a star. By killing my wife and son, I have taken the road toward the only kind of celebrity I can reasonably claim. Nothing but celebrity is worthwhile in the end.

We have a chance to be a movie because of me. My wreck of a family might become immortal. Thanks to me. Who would pass that up for a life of virtue? Meagerness is its own reward, too.

I cleaned myself and the wound on my arm and poured alcohol on it. That burned and sobered me too much and I drank some more of the bourbon, enough that I was staggering. I cleaned the knife with alcohol and bleach and laid it beside the sink. I knew I needed to leave but I wanted to rest for a while, I needed to close my eyes. I was feeling sick to my stomach. The blood smell spread all over the house. So I went into the family room and lay down on the couch for a minute.

"You bastard, you killed me," Carmine said from the floor.

"Yes, I did."

"Look at me. I'm a mess. I wet myself."

"You can't help it. Nobody's going to care."

"Are you just going to leave me lying here like this?"

"What do you mean?"

"You have a son. He's in there flat on his back. You don't even know if he's still alive or not."

"He's dead. I cut his throat."

"You don't know. You might have missed a part. He might be lying in there suffocating in his own blood, he might be suffering because of you."

"You never stop," I said.

She laughed. "That's because you never do anything right. Even my murder you screw up."

"You're dead, aren't you?"

"Yes, but you can't just leave me here."

"Why not?"

"Put something over me. I'm your wife, for pity's sake."

"I could cut you up into little pieces and put you down the toilet," I said.

"You wouldn't dare. God would curse you."

"God will already curse me for killing you in the first place."

"God would curse you even worse."

"I killed you and you won't even leave me alone," I said.

"Look at you, drunk. You're going to lie there and let them catch you, you're not even going to try to get away."

"I'm too drunk to drive anywhere."

"Make yourself a cup of coffee."

"Miss Know-It-All. Miss I've-Been-Murdered-A-Thousand-Times-Before."

"My mother will wake up any minute and walk out here and die of a heart attack."

"We should be so lucky," I said, and fell asleep for a while, and dreamed.

Child Abuse

I DRIVE TO THE ONLY PLACE I have left. I'll be on the road a while; Ann lives about forty minutes away, just across the state line in another town. I'm on the interstate headed toward a patchy line of skyscrapers. Traffic is moving in zooms and curves, and sleek German cars are darting in and out of lanes willy-nilly.

Doing my best to control my own narrative is not enough; I already wonder what I'm doing. I am already departing from my ideal dramatic arc. For instance, at this moment someone like O.J. Simpson should be driving, and I should be lying prone in the back seat of the car muttering about suicide. A briefcase with ten thousand dollars cash in the back of the suv would also be reassuring, although if I still had ten thousand dollars in the first place, I might not be in this pickle.

I thought I was making myself feel better by contemplating the idea of murdering Carmine, but when the opportunity presented itself the fantasy made the reality so easy. If I were being interviewed right now, I would say I was surprised at what I have done, that I never thought myself to be capable of anything like this, that I am just a normal person. I take out the garbage, I take a shower every morning, I play some golf now and then. But I have been thinking about killing Carmine this way for days and now I've done it. In the process I've also killed my son. It's even the case that I thought about that beforehand, too.

So now I'm a full-fledged, visible monster.

The memory of the moments when I was using the knife on the two of them are still coming back to me in flashes as I drive. The images are vivid and make me nauseous. I remember that I never even looked Frank in the face before I reached the knife across his throat; I remember that the knife bit into his cloudy neck without any effort and he never uttered any last word or expressed any surprise. Refusing to look at his eyes, I lowered the chair he was sitting in to the floor. I was surprised at my strength, that I was able to do it, but for God's sake I'm only fifty-eight, and I had no choice; and anyway, after the first cut, my adrenaline was flowing.

I get lost in that image and have to come back to my driving. I am still drunk enough that I need to pay attention or some state patrolman will pull me over and I'll never get to Ann's.

My shoulder aches from Carmine's nails in a way that pierces the fog, and it helps to concentrate on that. I have been favoring the shoulder on the drive but start to use it, despite the pain this causes, in order to keep my thoughts anchored in the car. There's still an ache in my gut. I'm still remembering bits and flashes of what happened and pushing them away: Carmine struggling hard to beat me off, tugging at my robe, scratching my shoulder, sure, at first, that she's strong enough to defend herself, until I stab her in the front and she cries out not so much pain as indignation. Pain comes later, when she grabs the blade of the knife and tries to stop me that way, blood dripping off her hands, but she refuses to let it go; this from a woman who if you pinched her would pout for days and complain of the ache and the bruising. In the last moment of her life she rose above so many things, even her fear of blood.

I sway off the road onto the exit ramp and the worst is over. On the streets I can go slow enough to blend into the rest of the mid-morning traffic.

Ann's car is parked in front of the apartment building. I roll out my suitcase from the car and carry it up the steps to her door. She lives in an old house that's been broken up into rental units; she got rooms at the back with a view of the yard. Nothing like the kind of house Ann was raised in, which we sold long ago to upgrade to the one I have just lost to the mortgage company.

When I knock, it takes her a while to answer. She's home from work at this hour of the morning so I know she's there.

"Who's that?" asks her roommate, the thin girl, Hilda.

"Ann's father."

There's a moment of something that should be silence but isn't, quite. I'm leaning my hand on a doorframe which has flaking paint of various shades of white and pale green, painted and repainted as tenants came and went, never sanded back to the grain of the wood and made fresh. I hear movement near the door on the other side. Hilda says, "She's not here."

"I know she's there. I know you're there Ann."

"I swear she's not."

"Shut up, Hilda. Ann, I'm sorry. I'm not going to hurt you. Please let me in. I don't have anywhere to go." This speech releases something that I've been holding in and a kind of sob rises out of me. "Please."

I can hear them talking inside. From the parking lot I can hear cars driving past and horns on the street and the openness of standing in the door this way makes me afraid. I am about to call her again when she opens the door. Her eyes are red, streaming with tears. "Gramma called," she says.

"When?"

"About ten minutes ago."

I stand there, saying nothing. Yes, I did this. Yes, I am the one. Here is the monster.

"Why did you do it, Dad?" she asks, her face collapsing.

When she calls me Dad I can feel something of the pain I've caused her. At the moment I have few feelings of my own, but I can feel some of hers. I say, "I didn't hurt anybody. I swear I didn't. I woke up and found them like that."

She's flooded with emotion, so much she can't speak. She's moving from foot to foot as if she's trying to reset her system, do a reboot.

"Are you going to let me come in?" I ask. "I'm begging you. I don't know where else to go."

"The police are on their way," she says. "They said you would come here."

"That's fine."

"You'll talk to them?" she asks.

"Yes. Sure."

"You really didn't do it?"

"No."

She's thinking hard, she's thinking for her life, for the first time. I can see a whole person rising up in her. She might say no to me, she might shut the door in my face. I want her to do that, I'll go away then, I'll keep driving. But the strong part of her is wavering; there is still so much weakness in her. She lets me in.

Her apartment looks upscale, full of her mother's castoffs. The living room is a mess but basically clean.

"You brought your suitcase," she says, as I roll it to the couch on the opposite wall.

"I don't know where I'll end up."

"Dad, you're sounding like you did something, or else why are you running. Did you?"

"You know they'll suspect me, Ann. Your grandmother already told you it was me, didn't she?"

Ann is pacing in her kitchen. Hilda steps out of the little hall that leads to the bedroom and glances at me and looks at Ann. She's concerned. She's alive right now, too. Maybe she's even hungry. "Is everything all right?"

"It's all right, Hilda. Leave us out here for a while."

"Are you sure?"

"He says he didn't do it." Ann is embracing herself, clutching her own shoulders, a soft blue sweater that clings to her round, full lower belly.

Hilda looks at me with her emaciated eyes. I know what she sees by her expression. I am a fearful thing, a lunatic, a possible killer. I try not to look at her too long. I study the copies of *Detail* magazine on their coffee table.

"Leave us alone," Ann says. "I'll call you if I need anything."

She has a monster in the room with her, Ann does. The sense of this is plain in her brittle calm as Hilda leaves the room; Ann paces and stays near the door. I put the suitcase on its side and unzip it and leave it there, watching my daughter. She is coming to terms with the shifting images that apply themselves to this strange world in which she suddenly finds herself, where everything is more real than usual, where her father might be a murderer, where he might have killed her brother and her mother only a short while ago. I am lulling her with the pleasant possibility that I did not do these crimes, and because it is a reality which she desires she bends toward it; but because she also, by instinct, feels I might actually be a monster, because the truth of that is in the cells of her body, in the air between us, she resists it at the same time and stays caught between both alternatives, unable to choose. She is becoming a whole person, I see her clearly. She can cope with this.

"What happened?" she asks.

"Come and sit down."

"I can't, I'm too restless. Just tell me."

"I woke up early this morning and your brother was there with your mother. We had breakfast together. I was still drunk from the night before and fell asleep on the couch. When I woke up, I found your mother and your brother dead." It is easier to refer to them this way, rather than use their names.

"Was it a robbery?"

"Your brother's wallet was gone. I don't know what else."

"Was there a door open?"

"The door to the pool. That's where your brother was sitting."

"Oh my God," she says, and sits on the opposite end of the couch.

I stand and walk between her and the door and the hall.

"You have to tell the police that," she says. "There's got to be evidence."

When she sees the knife in my hand, she stops. Her face changes. Her body collapses toward its center and a shudder of terror wipes out the rest of her. She's huddling, gathering her breath, getting ready to scream.

"Sit there and be quiet and I won't hurt you. If you even call out for Hilda, I'll kill you, and then I'll kill her."

She has a hard time controlling herself; I watch the changing emotions, terror struggling with a longing to cling to that possible world in which I am telling the truth about not hurting her. In which she will live if she does what I tell her to do. She grabs herself around the middle and holds her breath. "Please, Dad," she says. "Don't hurt me."

"You better not say anything," I tell her, and she nods, quickly.

"Everything all right out there?" Hilda calls.

"Tell her you're fine," I say.

"Everything's fine," Ann calls, her voice trembling. She has control of herself. She's studying me for any weakness. She no longer cares who I am, that I'm her father, except that she can plead using the bond, for mercy. She is gathered at another level of herself, a level that no longer cares whether she is my daughter, where she simply wants to live.

"I don't want to hurt you, Ann," I say, "but I have to do something."

The shock of fear again. "What? I'll scream. Hilda will call the police."

"No. Hilda will come rushing out here and I'll kill her and then I'll kill you, too."

She's breathing more heavily, but nods. "All right."

"You asked me a stupid question the other day. Do you remember?"

"I ask a lot of stupid questions."

"You asked me why I never abused you."

This sinks in and the new fear blossoms over her. She sinks backward against the couch slightly, tense in all her muscles. "I was joking around, Dad."

"You were?"

"Dad, if you touch me like that, I will scream. I swear."

I stand there with the knife. She's poised on the couch to move in any direction in the next heartbeat; she means it. She'll fight.

For a moment I might have done it, I might have attacked her. I can almost see it.

"Don't ever be that stupid again," I say.

"What?"

"To suggest such a thing for yourself. Don't ever be that stupid the rest of your life. Now, go back in the room with Hilda. Call the police if you want to."

She's breathing. She's trying to guess whether this is a trick.

"Give me the knife, then," she says.

"No. I keep that. You girls just stay back there and I'll sit out here and wait for the police."

"Please, Dad." She's starting to believe me, studying me with an intensity she never evidenced before. She's beginning to believe she may get out of this alive. Breathing with her abdomen, poised on her feet, sitting forward on the couch.

"I said I won't give you the knife, Ann. You told me the police are on the way. I'll just wait for them out here." I move toward her and she immediately slides away from me toward the hall. "Go sit with your friend."

"Why did you do it?" she asks.

I look at her. There's that feeling of a sob that should be here, a ghost of a sob. It needs to come out but I won't let it out. "I don't know."

"Were you quarreling?"

"Yes."

"Why was Frankie there?"

"He was trying to help your mother. She found out we were losing the house."

"Losing the house?" This knocks the wind out of her. "What? How is that possible?"

"Why do I still need to tell you that I'm out of work?" I say.

"I thought you'd have taken any old job you could get before you let that happen."

"You sound like your mother. Any old job won't pay that mortgage."

Sliding closer to that person I would like to kill, that daughter I would prefer not survive me, she becomes petulant and shouts. "No wonder she was divorcing you. No wonder she was sick of you."

"Don't do this, Ann."

"You could have said something. Frankie and I could have helped you."

"Your brother's idea of help was to schedule an appointment for your mother to see an attorney, and you've had your hand out to me for cash at every opportunity since you were eleven, so please tell me what kind of help you were going to be?"

She flushes red. "You didn't have to kill them."

I lunge toward her and grab her by the hair with the knife toward her throat. She whitens over with fright, her face pale, her lips trembling, drool brimming at the corner of her mouth. I shove her against the door and when Hilda appears I say, "If either one of you says a word or moves, I will cut Ann's throat wide open just like I did her mother. Do you understand?"

Hilda backs toward the door she came out of and nods.

"Stay still," I hiss at her.

She freezes and clings to the wall. I can see every blue vein in her thin, long arm.

Ann is trembling, tears in the corners of her eyes bursting into streams, little noises coming out of her throat.

"I don't know why," I say. "I crossed that line. That's all. Don't talk to me like I'm nobody, like I'm nothing."

She shakes her head, eyes closed, terrified to look at me.

"Never once in three years have you stopped to ask whether I could still afford to give you money, never once. You need to think better than that, Ann. You need to think a lot better."

She whimpers. I shove her down the hall; my shoulder burns when I do. She falls on the floor and looks at me. I am no longer certain what she might be seeing, how she might feel about it. She will have that for her future. She is the daughter of a monster, not quite human any more. Maybe that will be enough to save her life.

"Go in that room there, both of you. Close the door. If I hear the door open, I'll kill you both. Do you understand?"

Hilda nods quickly, nostrils flared. She helps Ann up and pulls her into the room. The door closes.

I put the knife in the bag and roll it to the door. I get out of there as fast I can. Nobody stops me as I pull the SUV onto the street.

Chances Are My Chances Are

I CHECK INTO A CHEAP MOTEL-ISH hotel along the interstate, nondescript, a room and a bathroom, a TV in a cheap stand. There's no news before noon so I won't know till then what my coverage is like.

In this barren room with two chairs and a queen bed I have to decide which kind of villain I have become. Am I the tragically stupid hero who stumbled into killing his wife through unfortunate throes of chance and ends his own life as soon as he comes to his senses? Or will I outlive my wife and son by a lot more than a day? The clock is ticking.

I test the hot water in the bathroom, run a tub full of it, get out the knife.

I have Carmine's purse, which has her bottle of Ambien in it. I can swallow those, drink the bourbon, get in the hot tub, cut my wrists as deep as possible, cutting carefully along rather than across the forearm; with this heavy knife I should be able to do plenty of damage, with the bourbon and Ambien to put me into a dreamy drowsiness and dull the pain. If I'm lucky I'll have time to die before the police figure out where I am.

If I'd planned better I'd have a gun with me but I've never owned one. In some ways, that would make the choice too simple and quick. With my luck I'd miss, anyway, and end my days as a paraplegic.

A decent man would do it, would end it here.

In the movie of my life, though, I might not present myself as much in the way of a decent man.

I scan the channels for a few seconds, a worshipful car ad leading to a male enhancement product leading to an pharmaceutical ad about a cure for toenail fungus that might kill you with liver disease, followed by beautiful Nicole Kidman selling Chanel and for a very good price, or so it appears, arresting images, every one. What star is there to help me now in my need? Ed Asner in his character from *The Mary Tyler Moore Show*? Alan Thicke from *Growing Pains*? Ellen DeGeneres on her new talk show? Ricki Lake?

No celebrity of any sort appears. Instead, it's Carmine in the corner, sitting in a chair with yellow vinyl upholstery, playing herself, dead. The bloody flap of cheek hangs down, and the nick in her lip makes her voice sound funny. "You know what you're going to do. Get on with it."

"You think I'll kill myself over you?" I blow out my breath. "You don't know me very well, do you?"

"I think you'll turn yourself in," she says. She really is smoking a cigarette in this take, sitting there in good light, the special effects working, the latex making her look like she's been sliced to pieces. "I think you'll get on the phone and call the cops."

"You think I'm that brave?"

She grins. It's really an ugly sight, but completely in character for her. "I think you're the same wimp you've always been, Charley. Killing me doesn't make you anything. You're still a dumpling."

I feel the clutch of hate for her in my gut that refuses to fade. "You're trying to push me into getting into the tub."

"It's going to run over soon," she says.

"I'm watching it."

"I don't know why you're bothering."

"Go to hell."

"Not a chance," she says. "I'll never leave you, darling."

I think about that. I turn off the tub and run my hand into the water. It's steaming.

"You can tell yourself you're staying alive for your daughter," she says. "Thanks to you, you're all she's got left. So you can say to yourself you're doing it for her."

Tears are welling in my eyes, genuine tears. "If you'd ever had an ounce of mercy in you, Carmine, you would have been the best woman in the world."

"I know you, Charley. You were drunk when you killed me. You didn't have the balls to do it sober. You don't want to die. You're about to piss yourself thinking about it."

I'm dizzy and sit on the bed. My hands and arms are trembling. The chair she was sitting in is empty now and she's nowhere else to be seen, but there's still her voice. "Pick up the phone, Charley. Stop wasting time."

I look for her and feel tears in my eyes. What I've done is so wrong, so complete and irrevocable, now that it's no longer fiction, now that I can't change it.

Her voice is so set and hard. "What do you want, you miserable piece of pork? You cut me into chunks and you want my forgiveness? Now that I'm dead I'm supposed to bless you? Fuck you, Charley. From beyond the grave, fuck you. Hate is eternal, Charley, it lasts just as long as love. I will always be here, I will never leave you, and from all the way back to the moment I met you I curse you. You are the scum of the universe to me, and I will hound you for the rest of your miserable days. Even if you don't want to survive I'm not giving you any choice. So pick up the phone and dial, my sweetheart."

I pick up the phone and dial. It takes a while, but I get through.

The noon news comes on and there I am, the cops around my house, the police tape, the earnest news reporter with outrageous hair. Shots of a stretcher covered by a sheet leaving the house. A shot of my frail, shaken mother-in-law. The police are asking anyone with news as to the whereabouts of the suspected assailant, Charles Ebenezer Stranger, please call this number and etcetera. For identification they're using my last picture from my days at Arthur Andersen. The images come to me as if from a distant planet, as if the story is about someone else.

I wait for a while. Every couple of minutes I think I need to pee and try and nothing comes out. There finally sounds a pounding on the door. "Police," I hear, and other words I can't make out, and my heart pounds. Uniform cops in body armor bash through the door and point guns at me. Detectives in suits come in, and more uniforms. The detectives look forceful and determined. My crime has caught their attention, they are energized, focused, striding in, looking around the room, while I'm being manhandled in the nicest way by a uniformed woman taller and heavier than me.

"The knife's over there," I say, pointing to a table across the room. "I'm not armed."

The guy detective grabs me anyway and the woman bends my arms behind my back and I feel joints ache from being twisted the wrong way. The shoulder burns from Carmine's scratches.

"Are you Charley Stranger," the detective asks.

"Yes."

"You live at," and he gives my address.

"Yes."

"Why you here in this cheap hotel, Charley? You want to tell us what happened?"

"You know what happened," I say. "I killed my wife and my son. Carmine Stranger and Frank Stranger."

"They were pretty cut up. What happened?"

"I had a fight with my wife. We were losing the house. She had asked for a divorce. She said some things."

The detective is nodding his head, listening, not responding at all. "What about your son?"

The woman is watching me without any sign of what she's thinking. The questions and their blank expressions are making me see, hear, what I'm saying, and it sounds so cheap, so ordinary.

"He was there. He would have stopped me from killing his mother."

The detectives look me over as if I'm hardly even there. This is nothing like a movie when I tell it, nothing at all. I'm a failed wreck of a human being who killed his partner and his child, one more vote for the dark side of the Force. I'm nobody. I've got my work cut out for me if I'm going to amount to anything as a criminal.

The woman recites my rights and they take me outside. There are reporters here from only two local TV stations but that's a start. The cops walk me past the reporters and cameras snap. I never try to cover my head, I'm true to myself from the first moment. Someone asks me, "Did you kill your wife and son, sir?" and I shake my head in weariness, looking stricken, as if I have seen too much. It is as if I can see myself in the lens of the camera, as if I can manipulate the image that is the final end-product, the picture of me that people will receive. Looking broken and penitent, I follow along beside the woman guiding me. The detectives shove me into the back seat of a car with my hands cuffed behind me. I make note of which television stations these are, and hope some of these people are real news reporters. I try to look willing to be interviewed. I'm going to need all the coverage I can get.

Epilogue

PRESIDENT BUSH HAD THIS TO SAY about my case, when he was taking questions on family values at a recent press conference at the White House: "I think if he's guilty of the crimes he committed, he should duly be punished underneath the law of, whatever, the state where he lives. That's the beauty of our justice here, you know. Even a criminal like this man will get his day in court. He's lucky he killed his wife in America. Next question."